THE
BLAIREAU
AFFAIR

OTHER TITLES BY ALPHONSE ALLAIS
PUBLISHED BY BLACK SCAT BOOKS

———

Captain Cap: His Adventures, His Ideas, His Drinks

How I Became an Idiot by Francisque Sarcey

Selected Plays of Alphonse Allais

The Squadron's Umbrella

Masks

THE
BLAIREAU
AFFAIR

ALPHONSE ALLAIS

Translated and with an introduction

by Doug Skinner

BLACK SCAT BOOKS
2015

THE BLAIREAU AFFAIR

by Alphonse Allais

Translated from the French by Doug Skinner

Copyright © 2015 by Black Scat Books

Translation and introduction © 2015 by Doug Skinner

ISBN-13 978-0-692-51952-3

FIRST AMERICAN EDITION
October, 2015

Cover & book design by Norman Conquest

ACKNOWLEDGEMENTS:

This novel was originally published in France in 1899 by the Revue Blanche under the title *L'Affaire Blaireau*.

Facing page: contemporary silhouette of Allais

BLACK SCAT BOOKS
Sublime Art & Literature
BlackScatBooks.com

"The first and last anarchist in France."
— Rachilde

INTRODUCTION

Alphonse Allais was born on October 20, 1854 (the same day as Rimbaud), in the northern port town of Honfleur. His family ran a pharmacy, and in 1872 young Alphonse was packed off to Paris to study the family trade.

Instead, he discovered the Bohemian life of Montmartre. He soon became a fixture at the cabaret Le Chat Noir; he contributed to its weekly paper, and eventually took over as editor. Collections of his short pieces started appearing in 1891. In 1892 he made the move to a wider audience, with his column *La vie drôle*, for the Parisian daily *Le Journal*. He was by then firmly established as a humorist, committed to several columns a week.

In 1895, he married the much younger Marguerite Marie Gouzée. Spurred, perhaps, by the need for further income, he then decided to write a play with Alfred Capus. Capus had published several novels and collections of short stories by then, and had a couple of moderately successful plays produced. The two men settled into Capus's house, near Blois, and set to work.

Playwriting was not as much of a departure for Allais as it might seem. Like many of his colleagues, he'd written monologues for the actor Coquelin Cadet, who popularized the form. He'd contributed to a few ephemeral revues, and often filled his columns with dialogues and playlets. And, not incidentally, he'd written a great deal of theatrical criticism for *Le Chat Noir*, usually appropriating the persona (and, famously, the byline) of the reactionary critic Francisque Sarcey.

Capus found Allais a difficult collaborator. Allais, after all, liked nothing better than to sit on the terrace of a cafe, drinking apéritifs and watching people go by; he had a habit of meeting his deadlines at the last minute. The writer Jules Renard noted a meeting with Capus:

"Yesterday, Capus, as bronzed as copper. He just finished a play with Alphonse Allais. It was hard to get Allais to work two or three hours a day.

"'To write a play,' Capus says, 'all you need is willpower and a spirit of sacrifice. In journalism, you can write a bad page today, as long as you write a good one tomorrow. With a play, you have to tear up the bad page. It was very difficult to get Allais to understand that.'"

Nevertheless, they finished a three-act play, *Innocent*, about the conviction of an innocent man, Blaireau, and the effect of this miscarriage of justice on a small town in the provinces. It opened at the Théâtre des Nouveautés on February 7, 1896, received lukewarm reviews, and closed after 29 performances.

With Capus's permission (and a percentage of the royalties), Allais turned the play into a serial, which ran as *L'Affaire Baliveau* in *Le Journal*, from August 6 to September 1, 1898. It was published as a book the next year, this time as *L'Affaire Blaireau*, by the Revue Blanche. (Capus, incidentally, went on to become quite a successful playwright indeed, and was admitted to both the Légion d'honneur and the Académie Française.)

The play fared better as a novel. Although Allais did paste in substantial swatches of dialogue, he rearranged the plot, and was able to enrich and develop the characters. The constable Parju, for example, made only a brief appearance near the end of *Innocent*; in the novel, he becomes a memorable presence. Allais also takes advantage of, as he puts it, "that admirable privilege that novelists enjoy to transport, instantaneously and without unfolding their wallets, their assembled readers to the most distant locations," to open up the action from the two sets (the country home and the prison) that theatrical production permitted. We can see Parju lose his badge, Alice write her letters, and Fléchard visit the public prosecutor, rather than hear other characters describe these interesting events afterwards.

For some reason, he also renamed all of the characters. Only Blaireau kept his name, after being redubbed Baliveau for the serial. As usual with Allais, many of the names are significant. Blaireau means "badger" (Baliveau is "sapling"), appropriate for the outdoorsy poacher. The amiable prison director, Bluette, is, aptly, a "trifle." Parju's name derives from parjure, "perjury." The hot-tempered mayor, Dubenoît, is "soft-spoken, sanctimonious," and his revolutionary rival, the lawyer Guilloche, evokes a repetitive pattern used as architectural ornament, and, probably, the guillotine. The judge, Lerechigneux, is identified, quite inappropriately, as "hesitant, indecisive." The Baron de Hautpertuis is a baron of a "high opening or strait"; however, his name also recalls Maupertuis, the mathematician who formulated the principle of least action, which certainly fits the easygoing Baron. The other names are not particularly evocative, unless I missed something.

With a title like *The Blaireau Affair*, contemporary readers were inevitably reminded of the Dreyfus Affair, which began making news in 1894. Capus was ardently Dreyfusard, as was the Revue Blanche, but Allais himself refused to take a stand. He was "neither for, nor against," and said "I have an opinion about it, but that's my own affair": as usual, he preferred to make a joke on the word "affair" than a serious statement. Although Allais was partial to anarchism, at least in his youth (Rachilde called him "the first and last anarchist of France"), he deliberately kept politics out of his column: "Social, economic, religious, military reforms, as much of all of that as you like; but for what is generally called *pure politics*, very little for us, please." There was, therefore, no partisan agenda in the novel: both conservative and revolutionary factions are made ridiculous, and Blaireau is lucky to be rid of them.

L'Affaire Blaireau has remained in print since 1899. I know of one Italian translation, by Enrico Piceni, in

1928. Despite its short life on the stage, its dramatic potential must have appealed to moviemakers; it was adapted to film no less than four times.

A silent version was made in 1923, directed by Louis Osmont, and starring André Brunet as Blaireau. Another version was made in 1931, directed by Henry Wulschleger, with Bach (Charles-Joseph Pasquier) as Blaireau. Bach also released a record of two songs as Blaireau: *Je suis brac* ("I'm a poacher") and *On n'm'a pas* ("Ain't got me"). Under the title *Ni vu, ni connu* (*Neither Seen, nor Recognized*), another version appeared in 1958, with Louis de Funès as Blaireau. And finally, a TV movie appeared on the series *Au siècle de Maupassant* in 2010, along with adaptations of stories by Hugo, Courteline, and other 19th century writers. It was directed by Jacques Santamaria, and this time Christophe Alévêque incarnated Blaireau.

Perhaps the most popular film version was *Ni vu, ni connu*. The role of Blaireau was expanded as a vehicle for Funès; one famous scene shows him winning a fishing contest, cheerfully reeling in fish after fish as the other contestants look on in bewilderment.

Blaireau's conflict with Parju was emphasized; in fact, Blaireau names his pig Parju. The heroically obtuse constable was played by Moustache (François-Alexandre Galepides), who also had the distinction of appearing in a short story by Boris Vian (so that Vian could point out how fat and hairy he looked in a bathing suit), and of being remembered by Georges Perec in *Je me souviens*.

Ni Vu, Ni Connu was famous enough to inspire a porn parody in 2015, in which a certain Stephano plays Blaireau, trading fish for sex. I've seen a clip, and can attest that Stephano does a suitably annoying impersonation of Funès.

L'Affaire Blaireau was Allais's only novel. A baffling thing called *Le Boomerang* was also serialized in *Le Journal* in 1903, under Allais's name. It was based on *Silvérie*, a one-act Allais wrote with Tristan Bernard, and his own one-act *Le Pauvre Bougre et le Bon Génie*, both based on earlier stories. It was ghost-written, as Allais cheerfully admitted, by whom nobody knows, and published in 1912. Another novel, *Dans la peau d'un autre?* (*In another's skin?*), appeared in 1907 under the names of Allais and Jehan Soudan. Viscount Jehan Soudan de Pierrefitte, traveling companion of Sarah Bernhardt and childhood friend of Allais, based it on one of Allais's stories, and prefaced it with a transparently phony letter from Allais.

So, this is Allais's only novel, and his longest work. It isn't quite as wild or cruel as his early stories, but I find it delicious anyway. Summer in the provinces, the shrewd but impressionable Blaireau, futile political squabbles, a ridiculous but charming love story, what more could one want? And innocence is rewarded!

Doug Skinner
New York City
August, 2015

A FEW LINES FROM THE AUTHOR, FOR THE BENEFIT OF TRISTAN BERNARD

Dear Tristan Bernard,

Do you recall the trip that we took, this time last year, to the grave of Chateaubriand? (I don't remember if the visit had the character of a pilgrimage, or was the result of a bet over a dozen lunches.) We boarded the train, following a pious custom, at the station in Montparnasse.

Evening, meanwhile, fell. I remember that as we passed the station at N., and as a sudden jolt warned us that we had crossed the first degree of longitude, I talked to you about my next book, with the warmth and volubility that characterize me in my periods of production. In my ardor, I committed myself to dedicating the book to you, subject to certain conditions.

Today I make good on my promise; not without great pleasure, I dedicate to you the following book, to which I draw your attention.

You will notice first that the descriptions in it are quite brief, and that I don't specify the general appearance of clouds, trees and various greenery, roads, wooded areas, waterways, etc., unless such details seem necessary to the intelligibility of the story.

On the other hand, the greatest care has been lavished on the "outline" (*dessin*) and the "color" (*peinture*) of the characters. In addition, the "plot" (*intrigue*) is woven with such skill that one might think it woven by machine; in fact, it was not. As for the "style" (*style*), it is consistently noble, and, thanks to a new filtration process, of a limpidity previously unknown.

Such, my dear friend, are the merits of this work, which, in exchange for this small courtesy of mine, you will recommend, a cigar at your lips, with authoritative nonchalance, in social circles, garden parties, and hunting expeditions.

Cordially yours,
ALPHONSE ALLAIS

(These few lines were written especially for M. Tristan Bernard; others, however, are welcome to read them, as they contain nothing confidential.)

$\mathscr{C}$HAPTER 1

In which we meet: 1. M. Jules Fléchard, a character who will be called upon to play a rather sizable role in the story; 2. A certain Placide, a faithful servant, but a protagonist, as (Henry) Bauër might say, of eleventh importance; 3. If the author has room, the very elegant Baron de Hautpertuis.

Madame de Chaville called:

"Placide!"

"Madame?"

"You may clear the table."

"Very well, Madame."

And Madame de Chaville left to join her guests.

Once alone, the faithful servant Placide grumbled the inevitable, "It's about time, I thought they'd never leave!"

He then seemed to hesitate between a glass of fine champagne and one of Chartreuse.

He finally opted for the latter, swigging a significant portion of it with obvious satisfaction.

Then, apparently changing his mind, he filled his glass with a very old brandy, which he sipped slowly, this time, like a true connoisseur.

"Well, M. Fléchard!"

A man was indeed crossing the garden, headed for the veranda, a man who appeared sickly and not particularly wealthy, but scrupulously clean, and not devoid of a certain elegance.

"Hello, Baptiste!" said the man who was not overly robust.

"Excuse me, M. Fléchard, not Baptiste, if you don't mind, but Placide. My name is Placide."

"It's a trifling detail, but if you insist: hello, Auguste, how are you?"

And the poor man dropped into a chair, with a discouraged, a very discouraged, expression!

"Decidedly, M. Fléchard, you are quite the stubborn eccentric!"

"One does what one can, my friend. Meanwhile, will you please inform Mlle. Arabella de Chaville that her gymnastics instructor is at her disposal."

"Her gymnastics instructor!" laughed Placide. "Ah, M. Fléchard, you can boast of giving me quite a laugh, that day that you introduced yourself as a gymnastics instructor!"

Without responding to all that was unseemly, insolent, and vulgar in the servant's remarks, M. Fléchard contented himself with mopping the sweat that poured from his brow.

I forgot to mention it, but there may still be time: all of these events take place on a torrid July afternoon, in Montpaillard, in the present day, on a sumptuous veranda giving onto a vast garden, or onto not very spacious grounds, *ad libitum*.

"A little glass of something, M. Fléchard?" Placide generously offered, no doubt to counter the poor impression left by his recent and inopportune hilarity.

"Thank you, but I only drink milk."

"A cigar, then? These are wonderful, and not too dry. I don't know if you're like me, M. Fléchard, but I adore cigars that are a bit moist. Besides, in Havana, where they're connoisseurs, as is only natural, they smoke cigars that are so fresh that when you twist them, juice comes out. Did you know that?"

"I was unaware of that detail, which means nothing to me, since I only smoke *nihil*, because of my bronchi."

The illiterate Placide seemed not to appreciate this joke from a lapsed academic, but, not to be outdone, added:

"Well, I only smoke the master's *puros*."

"Those are better than the *pooros* that you could afford."

This time, Placide understood, and burst out laughing:

"Go on with you, you joker!"

"And Mlle. Arabella, Victor, when will you trouble yourself to inform her of my presence?"

"Mlle. Arabella is playing tennis at the moment, with the young people. She's the liveliest of the bunch. What a crazy old lady!"

Jules Fléchard leapt to his feet; visibly offended by

Placide's remark, he glared angrily at the servant:

"I will appreciate it, my man, if you speak of Mlle. Arabella in more respectful terms, at least in my presence. Mlle. Arabella is not a crazy old lady. She is neither crazy, nor old."

"All the same, she's no kid anymore. Thirty-three years old!"

"She doesn't look it. And that's the important thing!"

Exhausted from this sudden burst of energy, the gymnastics instructor sat down again, his face streaming more and more, then, in a melancholy tone:

"So, do you think Mlle. Arabella will skip her gymnastics lesson today?"

"I tell you, when she's at her tennis, you could bomb the chateau, and it wouldn't even faze her."

(Placide liked to baptize as "chateau" his master's comfortable residence.)

"Well, too bad! I'll be on my way, then."

And Jules Fléchard turned that shade of pale and leaden gray that is a sure index of the worst moral distress.

Taking his hat in his left hand, then, our friend polished it with his right sleeve, more from mechanical instinct, we may assume, than in the hope of dazzling the townsfolk with his elegance.

He was about to leave, when a third character burst onto the veranda:

"Good day, sir, I... salute you! Tell me, Placide, has the postman come yet?"

"Not yet, Baron."

Meanwhile, Fléchard attentively studied the gentleman with the monocle, whom Placide had just greeted with the title of baron.

But no, there was no mistake. It was indeed he, the Baron de Hautpertuis!

"Baron de Hautpertuis, sir, I have the honor to greet you!"

The Baron (he was decidedly a baron) adjusted his monocle, his thick monocle, for the severely myopic, examined his interlocutor, then, suddenly joyful:

"What, you here, my good old Fléchard! Devil take me if I expected to run across you out here."

"I'm a shipwreck, Baron, and you know that ship-wrecks cannot choose their ports."

"That's true, shipwrecks cannot choose their ports, that's very true. But tell me, is someone at the Chavilles studying Dutch?"

"Dutch?" Fléchard asked with a smile. "Why Dutch?"

"Well, it seems to me," the Baron insisted, "that when I had the pleasure of meeting you..."

Fléchard struck his forehead and cried: "My word, Baron, I'd forgotten... That little episode had com-pletely escaped my memory... Yes, yes, now I remem-ber perfectly. When I had the honor of making your acquaintance, I was teaching Dutch to a young lady..."

"To the beautiful Catherine d'Arpajon. What a love-ly woman! Ah, the little imp!... By the way, Fléchard, tell me, what strange reason did Catherine have for learning Dutch? Dutch is not one of those languages that one takes up without a serious purpose."

"It's quite a story, Baron, which I can now tell you without indiscretion. Catherine d'Arpajon met, at the Auteuil Hippodrome, a rich planter who was quite generous, but knew not a word of French. When he left Paris, this foreigner, through an interpreter, told Catherine: 'My dear child, when you've learned the language of my country, come visit (my country, that is), and you'll be treated like a queen.' And he gave her his address. Shortly afterwards, I learned that Catherine d'Arpajon was looking for a Dutch teacher."

"And you introduced yourself?"

"Although I have my diploma," M. Fléchard added bitterly, "I found myself without a position; I introduced myself."

"You speak Dutch, then?"

"It was an opportunity to learn a few phrases."

"And the lovely Catherine, what happened to her?"

"I haven't seen her since. I only know that the poor girl was wrong about the language. It wasn't Dutch the planter spoke, but Danish."[1]

"And what are you doing now, Fléchard, old man?"

"I'm currently a gymnastics instructor."

"Gymnastics?"

Readjusting his monocle, the Baron de Hautpertuis lost himself in the contemplation of Jules's rather frail physique.

"Yes, Baron, gymnastics! Oh, I thought you'd be surprised."

"I must admit that your exterior doesn't especially mark you for that branch of education. How the devil did you come up with the idea?"

"Oh, my God! It's quite simple. After a number of failures, of all kinds, I became neurasthenic."

"How do you pronounce that?"

"Neurasthenic, Baron. The doctors suggested gymnastics, plenty of gymnastics, nothing but gymnastics. One two, one two, one two..."

"Excellent thing, gymnastics!"

"Excellent, yes, but here's the problem! Since my modest resources didn't permit me to practice the sport exclusively, I had the ingenious idea of supporting myself by teaching it... And so I set myself up as a gymnastics instructor."

"That's not a foolish idea, really, but have you succeeded?"

"In Paris, no, too much competition. So I came here, to Montpaillard."

"Hasn't your somewhat... feeble appearance discouraged your clientele?"

"Why, Baron? Not at all. To be a good gymnastics instructor, you don't need to be athletic yourself, just as you can teach accounting to perfection, without being a wealthy merchant."

"Your reasoning couldn't be bettered, my dear Fléchard."

"Besides, to avoid overwork, that terrible thing overwork, I recruit my students mostly among women and girls. Some have become strong — even stronger than me, which, just between the two of us, is not exactly an unbeatable record. And so Mlle. Arabella... Have you watched Mlle. Arabella on the trapeze?"

"I've seen her, but didn't really pay attention."

"You should have, Baron. Mlle. Arabella on the trapeze is the incarnation of Strength and Grace."

"I'm glad to hear it. The next time, I'll watch closely."

"Her performance is worth the trouble."

And Fléchard repeated in a kind of exaltation:

"Yes, Baron, the incarnation of Strength and Grace!"

"Why, Fléchard!" smiled the Baron. "What warmth! You wouldn't happen to be in love with your student, by any chance, like in a novel?"

"You're joking, Baron. In love with Mlle. Arabella, me, a humble gymnastics instructor?"

A platter filled with letters in his hand, Placide entered:

"The Baron's mail!"

"Will you excuse me, my dear Fléchard?"

"I beg of you, Baron. Besides, I was just leaving."

"I hope to see you soon, Fléchard."

"All my regards, Baron."

"Monsieur Fléchard," added Placide, "Mlle. Arabella asks you to return at five o'clock sharp for her gymnastics lesson."

"Ah!" exulted the poor lad.

---

1. For the reader ill versed in the art of geography, let us now learn that one of the Antilles, the island of Saint Thomas, is a Danish possession; the planter in question must have belonged to that colony. (Author's note.)

$\mathscr{C}$HAPTER 2

In which the reader will continue to make fascinating acquaintances, most notably in the Chaville family and among their guests.

Truly, one would have to be possessed by the devil to play tennis at that time of day, and in that temperature.

Fortunately, in the country, and even in many towns in the provinces, the autochthons enjoy an endurance far superior to that of us Parisians.

All the same, it was too hot, and the game was soon abandoned, by common accord.

Everyone headed for the veranda, where beer was served to the gentlemen, and raspberry syrup to the ladies.

While all of these people refresh themselves, let us examine them unobtrusively.

The masters of the house, first, M. and Mme. de Chaville, fine people, ordinary, wealthy.

M. Hubert de Chaville maintained, toward the end of the Empire, a long and rather riotous binge in the company of his excellent comrade de Hautpertuis, already mentioned. Then comes that terrible year, and our disasters. The young de Chaville valiantly does his duty as a lieutenant in the militia. The treaty of Frankfurt is signed. A few years later, our hero married an insignificant and wealthy cousin, who soon presented him with a girl, Lucie, who, at the time in which these events occur, had become the most charming young woman in the whole district. That is all.

The most interesting member of the family is, I may say without fear of contradiction, that Arabella de Chaville who was mentioned earlier, M. de Chaville's first cousin.

Since the faithful but discourteous servant Placide has already unveiled this person's age, we have no reason to conceal it: Arabella finds herself, in fact, in full possession of some thirty years of existence.

Does she look it? Jules Fléchard denies it, not without vivacity.

To contradict such a nice young msn would be criminal, so let us conclude gallantly: if Mlle. Arabella de Chaville *appears* to have passed twenty-eight years, that is the absolute limit.

We will even say "twenty-eight springtimes," to please Jules.

Despite her somewhat advanced age (for a young woman), Arabella has a heart that is forever young, an ardent heart, bored with beating through these days of platitude and dreary prose that we now traverse.

Rich, well bred, no uglier than any other, she had sworn to give herself only to a man who would sacrifice himself for her, a man who would face a thousand dangers, a thousand deaths, one of those men seldom encountered, alas, since the Crusades closed up shop.

The conditions were never met; Arabella kept her vow and remained single.[1]

When I say that the conditions were never met, I am perhaps too hasty, as the rest of the story will soon inform you.

Let us return to our guests.

The aforementioned Baron de Hautpertuis, an elegant Parisian rake, the closest friend of the excellent de Chaville, whom he visits every year for a few days in the summer. (Let us recall, and try to remember, that the Baron is as nearsighted, all by himself, as an entire wagonload of livestock. This detail will have some importance in what follows.)

M. Dubenoît, mayor of Montpaillard, and Mme. Dubenoît, his wife.

M. Dubenoît has only one obsession, but it is a good one: the tranquility of Montpaillard.

Since the founding of Montpaillard (at the end of the 16th century or the beginning of the 17th, historians disagree), revolutions have followed one another in France, thrones have crumbled, swanky heads have fallen under the blade of the guillotine, kings have discovered the path to exile, and the loudest uproars have troubled the peace of many cities, which deplorable excesses have sometimes even drenched in blood.

Alone, the little town of Montpaillard remained peaceful amid all of these upheavals.

"Since Henri IV," proclaimed M. Dubenoît with legitimate pride, "yes, gentlemen, since Henri IV, except for market days, there has never been the smallest crowd in the streets of Montpaillard."

And before the Baron's admiring expression, he insisted:

"Yes, M. de Hautpertuis, never the smallest crowd! And as long as I have the honor to serve as the high magistrate of Montpaillard, it will stay that way! I would rather see my city in ashes than a prey to disorder!"

"You're quite radical, Your Honor, for a conservative!"

It is M. Guilloche who issues this rather natural observation.

M. Guilloche is a young and elegant lawyer, who is one of the guests.

"When it comes to order, my dear Guilloche, one can never be too intransigent, and if you and your party ever try to trouble Montpaillard, you'll find me blocking your way."

"M. Guilloche has a party, then?" the Baron asked.

"Absolutely! You may contemplate in M. Guilloche the head of our city's revolutionary party, a party that boasts all of seventeen members. Whenever M. Guilloche runs for office, he receives eighteen votes in Montpaillard: seventeen from the revolutionaries, plus his own. The last time, he only got seventeen, because one of the revolutionaries was sick."

"Seventeen revolutionaries in a population of ten thousand!" the Baron exclaimed. "There is as yet no danger in the house. But tell me, my dear Guilloche, isn't it strange for a well-bred man like you to join such a party?"

M. Dubenoît interrupted before the young man could express his ardent love of humanity, his eagerness to sacrifice himself for the underprivileged. He cried out:

"Like all the rest of them, M. Guilloche is nothing but a careerist, one of those careerists who wouldn't hesitate to gather crowds in the street for a government position!"

"Excuse me, my dear Dubenoît..."

But meeting with the unanimous disapproval of the other guests, who were hostile to all political or religious discussion, the conversation turned to other topics.

Groups formed; Arabella chatted with the Baron:

"Mademoiselle," protested the latter, "I must permit myself to disagree. The little town of Montpaillard is by no means unpleasant, I can assure you. For the past week that I've been here, I haven't been bored for a minute."

"If you'd been here, like me, for... for some twenty years, you'd say otherwise. Well, what's done is done. I'll finish my life here among my cousins, like an old maid."

"Oh, mademoiselle!" the Baron protested gallantly.

"I'm talking about later."

"Ah, I see! Of course, eventually..."

"And you, are you returning to Paris?"

"For a few days, before heading off to sea."

"To rejoin your friends, your club, your mistresses..."

"My mistresses! How you do go on!"

"Don't deny it, it's natural for a man."

"Well then, say 'my mistress,' and let's drop the subject."

"Pretty?"

"Very pretty... and not after my money!"

"Think of me what you will, Baron, but I can't find it in me to blame those women."

"Nor can I," said the Baron.

"Their reputation may not be intact, but they're dishonored under such charming conditions! And besides, they lead lives of activity and surprise, whereas we... The ideal, you see, Baron, would be to reconcile the old family values of the provinces, with a somewhat ruined life... But it's very difficult."

"Eventually one finds a compromise."

"How many times have I found myself thinking about these things, as I walk through the grounds, alone and silent... My solitude oppresses me, my mind is lost in foolish dreams, a strange sensation steals over me..."

"And then what do you do?" asked the Baron, after a moment of silence.

Arabella let out a great sigh, and murmured, not

without a blush:

"I do gymnastics."

M. de Chaville approached:

"I'll bet that Arabella is telling you her troubles."

"Not at all. Mlle. Arabella has yet to take me into her confidence. I'm sorry for it."

"Don't listen to Hubert, Baron, he's only making fun of me. Besides, everyone here makes fun of me."

"They don't make fun of you, Arabella. They just tease you a bit because you're terribly romantic…"

"But," interrupted the Baron, "it's a fine thing to be romantic! Every woman should be romantic; me, if I were a woman, I'd be romantic."

"Of course, old man," added M. de Chaville, looking at Arabella, "but romantic to the point of feeding a prisoner in Montpaillard Prison for three months, of sending him a basket of provisions every day, with old burgundy and Havana cigars?"

"What, Hubert, how did you know…" said Arabella in embarrassment.

"Yes, of course I know, and I only mention it today, because tomorrow is the last day of his sentence."

"Will he be guillotined?" asked the Baron, with a shudder.

"No, simply released. His three months are over."

"I find this little adventure quite picturesque."

A blush of outraged modesty inflamed Arabella's features.

"I hope you won't tell M. de Hautpertuis…"

"I certainly will. I'll tell him the whole story, to your

great shame! Just imagine, dear Baron, that Arabella got all worked up over a sort of lowlife..."

"Don't believe a word, Baron!"

"And yet..."

(It would be useless to give the rest of the conversation, since the reader will find the subject developed further, not in the next chapter, but in one of the later ones.)

---

1. I probably shouldn't tell you this now, but, too bad, I just can't help myself. Know then that Arabella will get married near the end of the novel, and will be very happy.

$\mathcal{C}$HAPTER $\mathcal{VII}$

In which the reader will confirm that we did not exaggerate in the least, when, from the beginning, we introduced Mlle. Arabella de Chaville as being of a rather romantic disposition.

Poor Arabella!

Not only did she never meet the paladin of her dreams, but she searched in vain, not a single being into whose bosom she might pour the secrets of her ardent heart, of her dreamy soul!...

No one to understand her! Everyone, on the contrary, ready to laugh at her!

And in this existence that is always the same, eternally dull and flat, not a shadow of the tiniest adventure!

The only hints of an amorous life, of a passionate existence, she finds — but watered down by obvious fiction, by the writers' ignorance of their own heroes — in the novels or newspapers that come to her every day from Paris.

Oh! To be part of one of those dramas, even as a victim!

Oh! To have acid thrown in your face by a jealous rival; even that would be happiness! It would be living, at least!

Arabella is bored.

....

One day, a rather rare occurrence, there was a letter for her in the Chavilles' mail.

"I don't recognize the handwriting," she murmured, reading the address.

And she could not stop herself from trembling.

Although little versed in graphology, Arabella guessed that the handwriting on the envelope was from a man, an amorous man, an uncommon man.

Enigmatic instinct? Mysterious telepathy? What, exactly? We cannot know, but something, at that moment, informed our friend that this letter, this letter that was now burning her fingers, would have a definitive influence on her destiny.

Her heart beat quickly, and her hands shook so, that she had to wait a few moments before unsealing the disturbing missive.

Only three lines:

"Mademoiselle,

It is of vital importance that you know this: there is a man who loves you in the shadows.

DESPERATE"

Arabella closed her eyes; she thought that she was dreaming.

"A man who loves me in the shadows!" she murmured, in a voice much like Sarah Bernhardt's. "There is a man who loves me in the shadows!"

And the idea that a man loved her in the shadows, and that he was desperate, plunged her into the most ineffable of ecstasies.

But who could this tenebrous admirer be?

She sought the stranger in her usual circle.

So-and-so?

What's-his-name?

Such-and-such?

No, none of those three.

No one else, either.

Trembling with anticipation, she decided to await further developments.

The next day, a new letter of the same mysterious provenance.

The desperate man proclaimed that he was ever more desperate, that his love was turning to madness, but that, determined not to emerge from the shadows to which he had alluded in his previous letter, he would continue to suffer in silence.

The heated correspondence went on after that, to the tune of two or three letters a week.

The basis remained pure idolatry, but the form

often varied: sometimes savage despair, sometimes energetic resolution, with sometimes even "the need to finish all of this, one way or another."

Then, suddenly, one fine day, or rather one dark day, the eagerly awaited postman brought nothing more than newspapers, or catalogues from the great establishments of Parisian fashion.

Arabella waited.

Weeks passed.

The mysterious stranger had apparently retired into the most impenetrable shadows.

"Nothing for me?" Arabella asked the postman, with an anguish that she could scarcely conceal.

"Nothing, mademoiselle," the humble functionary invariably replied.

What had happened? What catastrophe had so brusquely interrupted this delicious and troubling correspondence? It was impossible that this man, this fiery lover, this desperate one, could have had his flame die out so suddenly! A flame doesn't die out without a reason! A passion doesn't disappear without having been satisfied, or, at least, without having been discouraged. Now, the stranger had not been discouraged; and on the other hand, had not been satisfied... "Come now," Arabella, trembling, continued to think, "why did he stop writing? Did he kill himself, as he wrote me in one of his last letters?"

She reread that letter. The need to finish it all one way or another was not a formal declaration; it must have been just a figure of speech...

And Arabella lost herself in conjectures, in reasonings, in hypotheses of all kinds; her imagination generated two or three novels a day, replete with the most tragic adventures.

$\mathscr{C}$HAPTER IV

Where different characters, destined to play a large part in the rest of this story, make a rapid entrance onto the stage.

It is a night with no moon, no stars, no planets: in short, no heavenly bodies at all.

Lamentable for a student of cosmography, such meteorological conditions in the firmament are welcomed by all gentlemen whose work risks certain dangers when undertaken, not only in sunlight, but even in the most discreet moonlight.

"Constable, be vigilant!"

Obedient to this objurgation, Parju (Ovide), village constable in Montpaillard, redoubled his vigilance.

This was, at the same time, both good for him and bad.

Good, if we adopt the attitude toward order cherished by his mayor, M. Dubenoît.

Bad, if we consider only the personal interest of

this humble functionary, who garnered, in the course of that memorable night, a severe manhandling, if I may say so, completely out of proportion with the modesty of his position.

Parju (Ovide) is one of those village constables cut from the same cloth that served France in that era when this great nation, respected outside its borders, prospered within them.

Only two beacons guided the skiff of Parju's conduct upon the ocean of duty: fanatic execution of the task assigned, whatever the task, and excessive veneration of all representatives of authority, whoever the representative and whatever the authority.

       ....

Please allow me a short but sage observation: if our poor dear crazy country contained only citizens like Parju (Ovide), there would still be bright days ahead for France!

       ....

On the day preceding this night so devoid of constellations, M. Dubenoît had met the constable.

"Good evening, Parju, anything new?"

"Nothing new, Your Honor."

"Perfect! Try to keep it that way. If there's still nothing new at the end of the year, I'll see that you get a bonus. Keep your eyes open, both of them, by night as well as day. Walk your beat, Parju, walk your beat by day, walk your beat by night, especially by night; good evening, Parju."

"Evening, Your Honor, you can sleep easy. I'll walk

my beat like nobody's business. I'll start tonight."

Parju kept his promise.

Leaving the order of the city of Montpaillard under the care of those numerous metropolitan officers whose duty it was, Parju targeted the urban periphery, or, to be less precious, the rural part of the district.

It was a dark night, as I said above, but an even quieter night.

From time to time, Parju stopped, listened like an Apache, and heard nothing but the tick tock of his massive and ancestral silver watch.

He continued his patrol.

And now he is next to the Chaville property.

Suddenly!... Aha!...

Suddenly, footsteps are heard...

A vague form is silhouetted against the dark wall surrounding the grounds.

Little by little, Parju's eyes have grown used to the dark.

Without a doubt, someone is trying to scale the enclosure.

"Got you, you damn tramp!" cries Parju, although somewhat prematurely.

In a single bound, like a panther in Java, he leaps upon the man, but without any great immediate advantage, for the aforesaid tramp has already offered the constable, and in less time than it takes to write it, a free show featuring thirty-six thousand stars, a show embellished with a few demonstrations of suppleness and strength, as the carnival posters say.

After which the mysterious intruder thinks it best to retire, without waiting for the cries, flattering though they always are, for an encore.

By the time Parju regained his senses, it was already too late to pursue the man whom he had somewhat severely called a tramp, for if the man were still running (a likely hypothesis), he must be far away, and in which direction? Good luck finding him!

The humble servant of public order remained nailed to the spot, prey to the most stinging humiliation of his career.

To be beaten? Oh, that was nothing! Is a soldier dishonored when wounded by gunfire? But what was serious, is to have apprehended the malefactor, and then let him escape, without even getting his description.

So rapidly, in fact, had the conflict occurred, that Parju could not have, in good conscience, indicated, even vaguely, the physical aspect of the gentleman.

(When I say "gentleman," you know what I mean.)

Fat or thin? Blond or brunette? Tenor or baritone? Cruel enigma!

And besides... but Parju could not let himself believe that in fact...

...It was too dark to look on the ground... but he would come back early in the morning... Oh no, he would find it... No, the Good Lord would not permit such a terrible thing!

And besides — we must say it, since it's important that it be known — shame of shames, the ultimate humiliation! Parju saw that his constable's badge had been torn off in the struggle.

His badge, the emblem of order! A constable who loses his badge, isn't that like a regiment whose flag is taken?

The sweat of disgrace pearled in fat drops on Parju's livid brow.

"But no," he wiped himself with his sleeve. "IT fell to the ground. I will find IT soon, as soon as the sun comes up."

Back home, he found a Mama Parju peevish at being awakened, more upset at the rips in his shirt than at the bruises on his face, and — sad to say! But women are like that — profoundly disinterested in the damage inflicted upon her husband's honor.

Chapter V

In which we make the acquaintance of the likable but unfortunate Blaireau, pale victim of an unhinged burgomaster.

Who was Blaireau, exactly?

No one could really say.

He was Blaireau, that's all.

Neither landowner, nor laborer, nor shopkeeper, nor manufacturer, nor state official, nor anything at all, Blaireau belonged to that class of creatures that are difficult to categorize, and seemed, besides, none too keen on filling a specific square on the social checkerboard.

Quite philosophical, quite crafty, this rural bohemian was suspected, by the populace, of balancing his budget (!) with transfers that favored local rabbits and other people's gardens, all simmered over dead (or live) wood, discreetly borrowed from the surrounding forests.

Blaireau obviously had quite a capacious bag of tricks, for no guard or policeman had ever succeeded in catching him *in flagrante delicto*, nor even issuing him the most innocuous ticket.

Twenty times, accused of various misdeeds, he had seen his rustic cabin, his modest bedding, his simple furniture, the object of judicial and intrusive searches.

The gendarmes found nothing except, sometimes, a rabbit of doubtful origin, or partridges of the same provenance.

"Where did you get this rabbit?" asked the sergeant.

"I bought it at market."

"Who from?"

"I don't know the lady's name. A big fat blonde with freckles all over her face."

"And these two partridges?"

"At the market too."

"From the fat blonde?"

"No, from a little curly-haired brunette."

"You would probably have some difficulty proving your testimony."

"Oh, sure! But the next time, I'll ask for a signed receipt from the sellers."

And before the puzzled stupefaction of the naive officer, Blaireau added calmly, but in a tone of perfect courtesy:

"Yes, sergeant, a signed receipt, and I'll have them add a ten centime stamp if my purchase equals or exceeds ten francs."

What could one say to such sarcasm? Furious at

seeing itself mocked, the force withdrew, not without a vengeful kick to some piece of furniture.

The gendarmes had not gone a dozen steps before Blaireau called them back:

"Gentlemen! A word, if you please!"

Then, indicating his poor topsy-turvy interior:

"And they call you," he smiled ironically, "representatives of order!"

Blaireau always had a joke ready, the pleasant outcome of all truly practical philosophies.

Unfortunately, Blaireau's philosophy did not prevent him from being the object of two fierce hatreds.

The hatred of the mayor of Montpaillard, M. Dubenoît, first of all, who refused to accept that an honest city like his could harbor such an irregular individual; then, and by reflection, the hostility of M. Parju (Ovide), already mentioned.

Whenever the conversation between the mayor and constable touched, by chance, on the accursed Blaireau:

"Well then! Parju, when can you lock up that scoundrel for me?"

"I'd like to, Your Honor, but he's as tricky as the devil!"

"I know, my friend, I know. Ah, if he were the constable, and you were Blaireau, he'd have arrested you long ago, my poor Parju!"

"Ah!" Parju laughed foolishly, "there's not much chance of that!"

Thus, when, came the dawn, Parju went to tell

M. Dubenoît about his nocturnal misadventure, the attempted arrest of a criminal, and the resistance of the latter, who left no address, but carried off the sacred badge, M. Dubenoît cried:

"All of that is pure Blaireau. Bring me Blaireau."

"But Your Honor..."

"Never mind the 'Your Honor.' Bring me Blaireau at once."

Parju offered a few more timid remarks, for, after all, arresting a man who actually has no charges against him, that's a serious business.

M. Dubenoît continued, with authority:

"Am I the mayor of Montpaillard? Or are you, Parju?"

"You, Your Honor, you're the mayor."

"Well then! Bring me Blaireau *illico*, I tell you. No one in this district but Blaireau is capable of such a crime."

"Yes, Your Honor."

"Go, Parju, do your duty. I'll take care of the rest."

And M. Dubenoît did indeed take care of "the rest," as he called it, so well that that poor devil Blaireau was, with unbelievable speed, arrested and sentenced to three months in prison.

Let us add that the mayor was powerfully assisted in this act of high justice by M. Lerechigneux, justice of the Montpaillard court.

As for Parju, he, duly prompted by the mayor, swore, without batting an eyelid, that he recognized his attacker. (Parju, let us repeat, knows nothing but duty.)

Blaireau, forgetting for the moment his usual philosophy, struggled like a devil in holy water, offered to provide an alibi, savagely protested his innocence, all in vain.

"Claims of innocence and alibis? That's how we recognize professional crooks. Blaireau, the court sentences you to three months in prison."

"Goddam it, damn it all, damnation and thunder! Really, this is too much1"

"Your foul temper, Blaireau, would lose nothing by expressing itself in less blasphemous terms. One more thing, Blaireau."

"What? Now what?"

"The court would have been happy to grant you a suspended sentence, in accordance with the Bérenger law, but we are of the opinion that you, on your own initiative, and for far too long, have already taken more than the country's entire judicial system would have given you."

"What? What does that mean?"

"Let me explain: despite all of your previous crimes, this is the first time that you've actually found yourself in contact with the court."

"Crimes! Me commit crimes! Never in my life!"

"My dear Blaireau, don't tell your lies to me! After all, I've bought game from you out of season more than twenty times! Guards, take away the prisoner."

And, laughing foolishly, the guards took away Blaireau, livid with rage.

CHAPTER VI

In which Silvio Pellico's lamentable record is in no danger of being broken.[1]

The prison in Montpaillard is what one might call a good prison.

The director, M. Bluette, a man still young, although having seen much of life, is in the first position of his administrative career, and his superiors are unanimous in predicting no future for him, given the extraordinary indulgence and humanity that he brings to his duties.

M. Bluette tried in vain, but was unable to see his prisoners as dangerous, or even contemptible; for him, they were simply unlucky, unfortunate, and he had met, on the asphalt of Paris, many scoundrels more threatening than the poor devils who were his guests.

Like all truly cultured men, M. Bluette is polite to

everyone, from the most abject of his prisoners to the most general of his inspectors, and if there were any difference, it would probably be in favor of the prisoners.

He was therefore adored by all of his charges, who went out of their way to please him.

His grand system consisted of setting his men to work on the occupations they exercised before their incarceration.

(Excluding, of course, the extra-legal activities that earned them conviction from the local authorities.)

At Montpaillard Prison, ex-carpenters do carpentry, and ex-cobblers make or repair shoes.

There was even, for a while, a former concierge who opened the prison door.

Untrustworthy, unfortunately, like many former concierges, he eventually opened the door for himself, and neglected to return, even though his sentence had not been fully served.

This little misadventure had no effect on M. Bluette, who continued to apply his system: as much as possible, of course, for difficulties often arose. For example:

"What did you do, my friend, before your conviction?"

"I was an aeronaut, sir, I made balloon ascensions at carnivals."

"Damn! I don't see how I can use you in that capacity, for the moment."

"The fact is that the ceiling is a bit low here."

And the man added, rather boldly:

"In the garden, over there... would that be possible? I'd be satisfied with a tethered balloon, of course."

"I'll think about it."

....

When Blaireau was admitted to M. Bluette's establishment, the latter was immediately charmed by the picturesque appearance of his new guest, who was thin, bony, with long arms like a monkey, and, in short, the general air of "a nice guy," due to his smiling eyes and his wide mouth studded with magnificent teeth.

On his way from court to prison, Blaireau had regained his composure.

Three months in the shade, well, so what? That never killed anyone. In fact, it promised to be a rainy spring, one of those foul springs more suited to staying in bed than walking in the woods.

All the same, that imbecile Parju who claimed to recognize him! He wouldn't let him get away with that when he got out! Oh no, he wouldn't let him get away with that!

He had three months of rumination to prepare a nice revenge, and he would come up with a superb one, damn it all!

Parju, you old scoundrel, just you wait!

....

M. Bluette asked Blaireau his usual question:

"Tell me, my friend, what did you do before your conviction?"

"I was a sort of handyman."

"Very well, my friend, you will continue to be a handyman here. In prison, there's always something for a handyman to do."

"I understand, sir," said Blaireau, totally won over. "I'll be a handyman to your complete satisfaction."

"I hope, my dear Blaireau, that during these three months that the government entrusts you to my care, we shall get along famously."

"I hope so too, sir... And besides, I promise that you won't be dealing with an ingrate. Do you like wild game?"

"Blaireau, our conversation is taking a dangerous turn... Let's turn to a safer subject: so, my friend, you beat up a policeman; that's pretty funny, you know."

"Pretty funny indeed, sir; but what's less funny is that I didn't beat up anybody, and was convicted anyway, for, just as I'm standing here, sir, I'm innocent."

"Oh no, Blaireau," cried Bluette, who, in spite of his general indulgence, found such a claim a bit excessive... "Oh no, please, don't start talking about a miscarriage of justice! I'm not interested."

"Well, fine then, all right," said Blaireau, who had regained all of his philosophy. "All right, I gave old papa Parju a good spanking, I ripped off his badge, and all the rest! Do you want me to confess that I killed Louis XVI while I'm at it? It's all the same to me!"

....

Intense indeed was Arabella's emotion when she learned from M. Dubenoît's own lips about the nocturnal drama on the walls of the Chaville grounds!

The mayor of Montpaillard could wander off onto the wrong track all he pleased, but she was not mistaken. She knew why a so-called criminal had tried to break into her home at night. Didn't one of the last letters that she received contain these words: "The walls of the grounds will not stop me"? And those words explained the drama. The walls of the grounds had not stopped him. Fortunately or unfortunately — Arabella could not quite decide between these two adverbs — the constable had halted an attempt that was, if not criminal, at least very daring.

The sudden cessation of amorous correspondence, following Blaireau's arrest, left no doubt in Arabella's mind. "Desperate" was obviously the audacious Blaireau, who had not shrunk from a nocturnal escapade! "The man who loved her in the shadows" was a poacher, well known in the area, whom she had often heard mentioned by the mayor of Montpaillard, but whom she did not remember having met. In any case, she could not recall his face.

This was, to be sure, a disappointment to our heroine, but she had to face facts. She sighed, thinking of the handsome, but somewhat vague, gentleman that her imagination had created from thin air, and who only lacked a name. Yes, she abandoned her novel with regret, but could feel no animosity toward the lowly worm who had dared to love her and to risk the chain gang to win her. (She preferred to think that he had risked the chain gang, rather than simply a few days in jail.)

"I cannot love him, of course, but I will not abandon him," she said to herself. "It would be odious for me not to interest myself in the fate of this poor boy, convicted because of his love for me. I must sweeten his captivity, especially because he showed such discretion, and let himself be convicted, when he could have been freed with a single word. It's too bad he's not a gentleman."

And that is why Blaireau received one morning, in Montpaillard Prison, a basket filled with exquisite provisions, ten bottles of wine, and fine cigars much like M. Chaville's, mentioned at the beginning of this story.

From that day on, the deliveries continued regularly.

Sometimes a perfumed note accompanied the basket: "Take courage!... All is known!... The person is grateful for your discretion..." etc.

Blaireau ate the provisions, drank the wine, smoked the cigars, read the perfumed notes, murmuring, "Who can this woman be?" and understood nothing.

In the meantime, he tended the garden, oiled guns for M. Bluette (who was a mighty hunter before the Lord), took care of the dogs, fabricated those thousand devices used in hunting and fishing, such as traps, nets, bartavelles, fishgarths, rissoles, rods, bowers, hoop-nets, lime-twigs, casting-nets, pannels, seines, dredges, net-strings, draw-nets, counter-buggers, libourets, trawls, etc., etc., a host, in short, of objects whose ingenious construction revealed in him a remarkable aviceptologist,[2] as well as a clever therionticographer[3] and an icthyomancer[4] of the first order.

Sometimes, M. Bluette asked him to catch a few gudgeons or other fish in the little river that ran through the foot of the directorial garden.

To say that it never occurred to Blaireau to take the passkey of the open country would be a fib, but he, a loyal soul, knew not to betray the trust placed in him, and could be seen returning regularly, his matelote or pan fry and he, at the appointed hour.

Thus passed the trimester, none too cellular, in fact, for Blaireau.

. . . .

In the morning, our captive rises, his heart filled with joy.

This is it, his last day of jail: tonight he will sleep under the bright sun of freedom, if you will excuse the expression.

Blaireau is radiant...

Alas, Blaireau, it is written that you have not yet attained the peak of your terrible Calvary!

---

1. Let no one complain about the inaccuracy of the following description!
In fact, many departmental prisons resemble family hotels more than harsh jails. (A. A.)
2. *Aviceptologist*, a man skilled in the taking of all kinds of birds.
3. *Therionticographer*, a person who, without having written a treatise on the art of hunting (*theriontics*), is nevertheless ignorant of none of its secrets.
4. *Icthyomancer*, an individual who claims to divine the future based on the behavior of fish.

CHAPTER VII

In which a drama which had remained totally obscure until now will appear as limpid as a mountain spring.

Let us return, if you please, all of you ladies and gentlemen who do me the honor of reading me, let us return to the Chaville house, to those grounds in the heart of which was laid the beginning of our story.

It is now five o'clock, and the mercury in the thermometer has returned to a lower and more reasonable level.

While the Chaville family and their guests chat about this and that, Mlle. Arabella joins her gymnastics instructor, M. Jules Fléchard, who has been waiting for her for several minutes.

"Good day, M. Fléchard."

"Mademoiselle Arabella, I have the great honor of greeting you."

"Please forgive me for making you come back, M.

Fléchard. We had company..."

"I know, mademoiselle, but it doesn't matter... The important thing is that I returned. I thought for a moment that you wouldn't take your lesson today, and was deeply disappointed."

"You're disappointed for so little, M. Fléchard. A missed lesson is not important."

"Excuse me, mademoiselle, but for me, it's quite important."

"I don't see why, since you're paid by the month."

"Ah, mademoiselle!"

And laying both hands on his heart, Fléchard tottered, as if he had received a deathblow straight to the chest.

"What? What's the matter?" asks Arabella, worried.

"The matter, mademoiselle, is that you have just wounded me."

"Me?"

"Yes, you, mademoiselle. You have just caused me one of the greatest sorrows of my life!"

"But M. Fléchard, please, explain yourself!"

Jules Fléchard has apparently recovered:

"It's not worth the trouble, mademoiselle. Let's drop the subject, if you please, and get to work."

"M. Fléchard, I insist that you tell me what's wrong with you today. You're acting so funny!"

"No, mademoiselle, I'm not acting funny, you're mistaken, and there's nothing wrong with me. (*In a bitter tone.*) And besides, do I have the right to have something wrong with me? I'm paid by the month!"

Arabella was very sorry; she had apparently upset the poor boy:

"My dear M. Fléchard, you may be assured that I didn't say that to offend you."

"To offend me! How can one offend a man who's paid by the month!"

"I have the greatest respect for you, and would never forgive myself if I caused you any pain."

"By the month! Paid by the month!"

"But what dishonor is there, M. Fléchard, in being paid by the month? Ambassadors are also paid by the month."

"With the difference, mademoiselle, that they're paid much more."

"Oh, what do salaries matter? All positions are honorable when filled by men who are intelligent and distinguished... like you, M. Fléchard."

"So you say, mademoiselle, and I thank you for it. It doesn't prevent the fact that you would accept from an ambassador many things that you would never accept from a gymnastics instructor."

"Don't believe it! I'm not one of those prejudiced women."

"Oh, oh!"

"I swear to it, M. Fléchard, and (*with an air of mystery*) perhaps you will soon see that it's true."

"Well, mademoiselle, let me offer you a little supposition, a tiny little supposition, with your permission."

"You have my permission."

"Suppose that a man, in an inferior position (and despite what you say, there are inferior positions), let us suppose that this man dared to lift his eyes to a woman... like you, mademoiselle."

"And?"

"Let us suppose that he even permits himself... to love her! And that's where we see that there is indeed a difference, between him and an ambassador!"

"None whatsoever, as far as I'm concerned. First of all, I could only love a man who was as romantic as myself, capable of heroic and dangerous exploits, in a word, a man not like the others! And whether that man be an ambassador or a gymnastics instructor, I will be his wife!"

They were lovely to see, both of them: the mature woman trembling with a sort of noble exaltation, the gymnastics instructor with fire in his eyes, fire kindled by, who knows? By his highest hopes!

Fléchard continued:

"And so, mademoiselle, you would love a man who risked imprisonment for you, who risked dishonor?"

"At once!"

"A man who, for you, came close to killing someone?"

A veil of sorrow passed over Arabella's features.

"Ah, hold your tongue, M. Fléchard. You remind me of that man who, just to glimpse me for a second at my window, almost knocked a constable unconscious, and who now shivers in a cell... until tomorrow."

"Blaireau! Are you talking about Blaireau?"

"Of course."

And you assume that this Blaireau tried to climb the wall of the grounds just to see you?"

"Obviously... At the hearing, they said it was to steal chickens. But I know better, I know all about it!"

"And so?"

"And so... nothing... I merely sweetened his captivity by sending him a few little treats, like jam."

Fléchard started:

"Jam!"

"Wine..."

"Wine!"

"Cigars..."

"Cigars!"

He muttered, "That filthy Blaireau," then:

"And what did he say, this Blaireau, when he received all of these delicacies? He accepted them?"

"I have every reason to believe that he did."

"He ate the jam? He drank the wine? He smoked the cigars?"

"Of course!"

"And the director of the prison tolerated all this gluttony?"

"M. Bluette is very kind to his guests."

Jules Fléchard stood up like a man who has just made a virile resolution.

"Mlle. Arabella de Chaville, I have something extraordinarily important to communicate to you."

"My God, what's the matter?'

"This Blaireau in whom you seem to take such an interest, this Blaireau is an impostor!"

"What do you mean?"

"This Blaireau," Fléchard continued forcefully, "had no right to your jam, nor to your wine, nor to your cigars; this Blaireau had no right to the slightest courtesy from you."

"I don't understand."

"This Blaireau is a scoundrel!... He's innocent!"

"Innocent?"

"Absolutely."

"You're mad, Fléchard!"

"No, mademoiselle, I am not mad. 'The man who loves you in the shadows' is not he."

"'The man who loves me in the shadows'! How do you know the words from those passionate letters?"

"I know them, mademoiselle, because it was I who wrote them!"

"You?"

"Do you remember the letter beginning with: 'You who are a soul of the elite' and ending with: 'I am consumed by love,' and that other one where I told you: 'Three times a week, I suffer a little less.'"

"Yes, I never understood what that meant."

"Those were the three times a week that I gave you your gymnastics lesson."

"My God! My God! And so, my poor Fléchard, it was you all along?"

"It was I, mademoiselle, I who never hesitated for a second to let an innocent man be convicted in my place, so that I might still see you, hear you..."

"And it was you who knocked out poor Parju? Who would have believed it?"

"Oh, I may appear slender, you know, but I'm energetic, terribly energetic! That night, I could have killed ten men!"

"Why did you stop writing me after that?"

"Remorse... Fear of compromising you... Who knows?"

"And so, the mysterious stranger..."

"It was I... And now, mademoiselle, all that remains is for me to beg humbly for your forgiveness... and to leave, I suppose."

There was a silence.

Both of them, their eyes lowered, seemed to be controlling their emotions. As Fléchard started for the door, Araballa ordered in a low voice:

"Stay, Fléchard."

Fléchard kissed the hand that she offered.

CHAPTER VIII

*In which, thanks to the hostile attitude of a fanatic for order, several
devout individuals cannot find a single poor victim to comfort.*

Let us be discreet.

Let us, if you will be so kind, leave these two tender
hearts to commune under the shadow of the trapeze,
and let us return to the grounds, to mingle with the
guests.

The Baron de Hautpertuis is surrounded by young
men and women.

The young men are admiring the distinguished
Parisian's outfit, so sober and yet so elegant.

Oh, that tie! Oh, the cut of that jacket! Oh, the cord
on that monocle!

And they fall into a reverie, those fine young men!
Ah, Paris! Decidedly, only in Paris do men know how
to dress.

The young ladies lavish the Baron with the most

delicious smiles that their twenty summers can offer.

They have something to ask him, but none dares be the first to risk it.

"You, Lucie, ask him!"

Lucie makes up her mind, and, not without a charming awkwardness:

"If you were very nice, Baron," she says, "do you know what you would do?"

"My dear child, if I didn't do all that I could to be agreeable to you, I would be quite a hideous monster indeed."

"Well, then! You would organize something for us."

"Organize something for you? That's a rather vague plan, Mlle. Julie."

"A gala or something, a nice gala, like in Paris."

"Something for charity, for example?"

"Yes, that's it, a gala for charity, here on the grounds."

"An excellent idea! But for whose benefit?"

"We don't know yet, but we could easily find someone."

"Don't be so sure, mademoiselle, it's sometimes quite difficult to find victims — I mean victims for charity galas."

"Oh! In the country, we're less choosy than in Paris."

"Mademoiselle, I am happy to place myself at your disposal. We shall organize the very best thing of its kind, a gala that will revolutionize the whole countryside!"

"Revolutionize the whole countryside!"

M. Dubenoît had just heard that terrifying phrase: "Revolutionize the countryside!"

"Stop right there, Baron! Revolutionize Montpaillard? Don't even think about it!"

"Oh! With a charity gala."

"With a charity gala, or any other ceremony, peaceful cities must never be troubled. Now, Montpaillard is the most peaceful community in France, and as long as I have the honor of being mayor..."

"Yes," interrupted Guilloche, "we know the rest. It's not the city of Montpaillard that should have elected you mayor, M. Dubenoît, but an oyster bed!"

"I prefer that to leading a city in chaos. And besides, a charity gala for whose benefit?"

"Why, for the poor of the region," proposed the Baron.

"There are no poor of the region. Everyone is reasonably well-off."

"Did you ever have, a while ago perhaps, some catastrophe?"

"A catastrophe? There has never been a catastrophe in Montpaillard, and as long as I'm mayor..."

"There will be no catastrophe, I understand. What about an epidemic, did you ever have a little epidemic?"

"Never!"

"Damn, too bad! And victims of the harsh winter, did you have any victims of the harsh winter around here?"

"Winter claims no victims in Montpaillard... On the contrary."

"No luck there... What if we built an old people's

home?"

"We have one that dates from Vauban, and it's still as good as new."

"Quite regrettable! Let's keep looking."

"Look as much as you like," persisted M. Dubenoît, "Look, and you'll find nothing. There are no victims of any kind in Montpaillard."

"Well then, we'll just have to organize our gala for the benefit of foreign victims. I organized one myself, I who speak to you now, for the victims of the Niagara fire."

"The fire?... Don't you mean the flood?"

"No, no, the fire, don't you remember that catastrophe?"

"Heavens, no."

"And yet it caused a sensation at the time."

"I can well believe it."

"Well, come now, let's keep looking."

ℭHAPTER ⁓ IX⁓

In which Jules Fléchard finds a hair in the azure of his firmament.

What a funny life this is, all the same!

Years — sometimes — follow one another, succeed one another automatically without bringing anything new to your destiny, unless it be to clip, a bit every day, the plumage of that stupid and charming bird that we call Hope; and then, all of a sudden, in an instant, everything changes!

The swamp of your monotonous existence is brusquely transformed into a raging sea.

Lights flash in the dull gray of your firmament, and wings, it seems, sprout from your scapulas.

Such were the reflections that agitated the mind of Arabella de Chaville, after the dramatic revelations recounted so poignantly in an earlier chapter.

So then, she was loved!

Loved as she had always dreamed of being loved, in romantic circumstances, by a man who did not hesitate, at night, to leap over the walls of the grounds to glimpse, if only for a second, the dim silhouette of his beloved, behind a curtain!

Loved by a man who trounced the watchman, like in the good old days of medieval adventure!

And, discreetly, between two pull-ups, Arabella contemplated her instructor.

Certainly, at first sight, one would never take Jules Fléchard for a man of action, but, on further consideration, your astonishment would cease.

His brown eyes are those of a lover, and his general air of fatigue reveals a hero temporarily weary of his long struggles with Destiny. One senses that his arms have been broken, as Baudelaire said, "while embracing the clouds."

That, at any rate, was the vision that came to Arabella.

Several times, the eyes of our two heroes met, and happiness could be read therein, and hope.

The half hour struck in the nearby belfry: the moment when the gymnastics lesson came to an end.

Standing erect, in that stiffness affected by those who make a a sudden decision, Arabella took the hand of her instructor:

"Farewell, my dear Fléchard, and be assured that I shall not forget you during the time that we must be separated!"

"Separated?"

"Alas, yes! While you are in prison, my friend."

"In prison?"

Poor Fléchard suddenly looked worried. Arabella was not going to insist that he turn himself in, now! That would be a little too romantic.

"In prison?"

"But however severe the judges may be, my dear friend, you have already been acquitted in the court-room of my heart."

"Do you really think it would serve a purpose, ma-demoiselle, if I turned myself in?"

"You must!... What is more beautiful than to face trial and imprisonment for the woman you love!"

"Yes, in fact, it is beautiful, very beautiful! But you know now that I would face them, right? That's the important thing! Let's remember that, the two of us, and speak of it, if you like, from time to time, but why shout it out to everyone?"

"You must follow the sacrifice through to the end, Fléchard!... And besides, that poor Blaireau is inno-cent. Give him back his reputation..."

The instructor permitted himself a laugh:

"Oh, Blaireau's reputation! I'll give the man a few hundred sous, he'd be happier with that!"

"No weakness, Fléchard! Turn yourself in with that heroism that suits you so well, and which I find so at-tractive in you!"

"But won't it seem pretentious? Won't it seem like — if you will pardon the expression — grandstand-ing?"

"No, Fléchard, you will seem to be doing your duty, and will emerge from the ordeal a greater man, especially in my eyes."

Obviously, he had to bite the bullet! All the same, it was a peculiar idea to make him go to prison... But, bah, he'd get out of prison! And after that, oh rapture!

"Mlle. Arabella, you have convinced me!"

"It's about time, Fléchard! I'll summon the proper authorities, and you'll repeat what you just told me."

"That I love you?"

"No, that's none of their business: that you are guilty, and that Blaireau is innocent."

Fléchard had one more hesitation:

"And what if we put off that little ceremony for a while?"

"Oh, my friend!..."

"Very well, mademoiselle. Please summon the authorities. I am ready for the sacrifice."

"Bravo, Fléchard!.. And hold yourself proudly!"

*C*HAPTER X

In which Fléchard publicly rends the hideous veil of misunderstanding.

Arabella was not gone long.

She soon returned with several gentlemen, who seemed intrigued by her air of mystery.

In the group were M. de Chaville, the Baron de Hautpertuis, M. Guilloche, M. Lerechigneux, the judge, and, visibly upset, the mayor, M. Dubenoît.

M. de Chaville spoke first:

"What is it, Fléchard? You asked for us?"

"Yes, gentlemen, I want you to hear a serious communication that I have to make."

"A serious communication?"

"A serious communication! Besides, I see among you the honorable judge, M. Lerechigneux; I'm glad of that, since his presence here will give greater weight to my declaration."

It was a solemn moment...

Fléchard coughed and continued:

"Gentlemen, the Blaireau affair is probably still fresh in your minds?"

"Yes," exploded M. Dubenoît, "Blaireau, the worst poacher in the whole country, a bad egg that our honorable judge here let off too lightly!... Three months in prison, I ask you! And to think that he served his sentence, and will soon be free! But he'll have me to deal with!"

"Very well, gentlemen, Blaireau was not guilty, Blaireau was convicted unjustly."

Had lightning suddenly struck those gentlemen, their surprise would certainly have been more considerable, but, even so, they were still astonished at this declaration.

"What's all this nonsense, Fléchard?"

"It is not nonsense, gentlemen... I swear to it, for in this shadowy Blaireau affair, the true guilty party, as I have just had the honor and the pleasure to confess to Mlle. Arabella de Chaville, is your humble servant."

Dubenoît became more and more alarmed.

A miscarriage of justice in Montpaillard, well! That's all he needed! The seventeen local revolutionaries would take advantage of this to create disorder!... No, it was impossible, and His Honor the mayor appealed to His Honor the judge.

The magistrate took the whole thing more calmly.

"The Blaireau affair? Yes, I remember it well. A poacher, wasn't he? A fellow who protested that he was innocent, and said he had an alibi... But, as I firmly reminded him at the time, alibis are how we can tell that someone is really guilty. Have you ever known an honest man to resort to an alibi, or even to mention it?"

"True," added Dubenoît, "very true!"

"Besides," continued the judge, "if M. Fléchard can prove that he's guilty, we'll convict him, just as we convicted Blaireau, who couldn't prove his innocence."

"You wouldn't do that, M. Lerechigneux! In the name of public order, in the name of the peace of Montpaillard, I beg of you!"

M. Guilloche beamed.

A miscarriage of justice! Ha ha! They'd have a good laugh over that! And the public authorities could get ready to spend an unpleasant quarter of an hour.

"Yes, Your Honor," snickered the ambitious youth, "it's not about the peace of Montpaillard right now, but something more important."

"Leave me alone! You can see that Fléchard, for some reason that I don't understand, is just fooling with us. The constable positively identified Blaireau as his attacker."

"The constable was absolutely wrong, that's all!"

Fléchard drew from his clothing an object which he unwrapped with the greatest care:

"Do you know what this is?"

"What is it?"

"Take a look, gentlemen. This is the constable's badge, the badge that I tore from him in the struggle!

It is the badge that commemorates my remorse, and I always carry it with me."

"A funny idea!"

"See, gentlemen, I engraved the date on it."

Guilloche was triumphant.

"There can be no doubt now. We find ourselves in the presence of an incontestable miscarriage of justice, one of the finest miscarriages of justice that I have ever encountered in my legal career."

But the honorable M. Dubenoît didn't see it that way.

"A miscarriage of justice! Never!"

"And what is it then, may I ask?"

"A little misunderstanding, a simple misunderstanding not worth our attention for more than five minutes."

"Ah, is that so?"

"Your Blaireau is nothing but a bad apple! Even if he wasn't guilty in this particular affair, he has on his conscience a host of other crimes for which he was never convicted."

"That's no excuse."

"I beg your pardon, but it is, and an excellent one at that! Blaireau is an admitted poacher. You can't tell me otherwise, I'm one of his best customers... when the season is over. And this is the character that you want to set up as a victim, as a victim of a miscarriage of justice!"

At the word "victim," the Baron de Hautpertuis came to attention.

"A victim! But there's our victim! And you, Your Honor, who insisted that there were no victims in Montpaillard!"

"Excuse me, Baron, excuse me..."

"Victim of a miscarriage of justice! This will be my first charity gala for the benefit of a victim of this kind. I've had victims of fires, victims of floods, victims of cholera, but never victims of the judiciary."

Everyone, even and especially Judge Lerechigneux, had to laugh.

"That will complete your collection, my dear Baron!" said the impulsive magistrate.

A bit annoyed that nobody was paying attention to him, Jules Fléchard declared solemnly:

"And now, gentlemen, I must leave you. I shall go unburden myself into the bosom of the public prosecutor."

"You will not!" cried Dubenoît. "You will not, Fléchard! Come now, my friend, just think, you'd unleash a storm of blood and fire in Montpaillard!"

The mayor's alarm brought the young lawyer unbounded joy.

"M. Fléchard knows nothing but his duty as an honest man. Right, Fléchard?"

"And I shall fulfill it to the end, come what may!"

A passionate look from Arabella compensated the hero, who did not hesitate to place his left hand on his heart, as a gesture of civic courage and sacrifice to duty.

M. Guilloche had donned his hat.

"Would you like me to be your lawyer?"

"With pleasure."

"Let's go, then. I'll accompany you to the public prosecutor's office."

"Goodbye, gentlemen. Goodbye, mademoiselle."

In a voice that was more and more Sarahbernhard-tesque, Arabella let fall these words:

"Goodbye, my friend, and take courage."

M. Dubenoît collapsed onto a bench.

"A miscarriage of justice in Montpaillard! Ah, this will turn out nicely!"

And the Baron de Hautpertuis rejoined the young people to tell them the good news:

"A victim, ladies! A victim! We have a victim!"

"Tell us about it, Baron!"

And all of those young folks clapped their hands.

"Just imagine, ladies..."

(For the rest, see above.)

As for Jules Fléchard, it was in a starry dream that he entered the office, murmuring:

"What a tone of voice that was when she said: 'Goodbye, my friend, and take courage!'"

Chapter XL

In which the author puts his clientele in contact with a young and elegant woman of irregular morals, but not devoid, incidentally, of worthy sentiments, which is more often the case than one might think with such a creature.

Ladies and gentlemen, all my readers, into the car!

Using that admirable privilege that novelists enjoy to transport, instantaneously and without unfolding their wallets, their assembled readers to the most distant locations, I shall, for a few hours, tear you from the delightful township of Montpaillard, where we have just spent together some ten... chapters.

So, here we are in Paris.

In the Étoile district.

In a cozy little apartment occupied by a young woman, one of those young women who... one of those young woman of whom...

This person who is not a young girl, because she is a young woman, as I said, is also not the wife of some individual.

Widow? Not in the least.

And besides, it would be inelegant to insist upon this inquiry, which is perfectly unnecessary anyway, and more suitable for some mercenary working for the census, because the lines that follow will establish soon enough the regrettable civil status of the pretty little sinner.

At the moment that we broach her threshold, the little lady does not look happy. With a furious hand, she crumples the missive that an amiable chambermaid has just given her.

Continuing to use my aforesaid privilege, I shall translate into clear language the thoughts that agitate this little lady's little soul.

Her friend, her principal friend — for who doesn't have her gigolo? — her serious friend, M. de Hautpertuis, had promised that he would return to Paris that very day.

After which, it was off to Trouville. And then, all of a sudden, now the gentleman is asking her to be patient a little longer.

He's having such a good time, he is, out in the country, with his old pal de Chaville, he's so spoiled, so pampered!

And besides, the young women in the provinces are so sweet! It's a bit of a change from the Jardin de Paris, don't you think, and the Bois de Boulogne, and the Palais de Glace.

All of the Baron's letter was conceived in those terms.

"Ah, you like a bit of a change, you old fool!" raged the little lady. "Well, so do I! Ah, you like it in Montpaillard, do you? Well, I'll go there myself! As a matter of fact, I know someone there too... Augustine!"

"Madame?"

"Pack me a bag, just a little one, for a few days... Nothing but the essentials..."

"Very well, madame."

"A simple and sober outfit is just the thing for where I'm going... To prison! Oh, this will be fun, my God, this will be so much fun!"

She took two sheets of paper and two envelopes.

On the first sheet she wrote, in beautiful English penmanship, tall, straight, and firm, these words:

"My dear friend,

"You must delay, you tell me, your return to Paris for a few days. It could not have happened at a more opportune time, for I have just received troubling news about the health of my aunt in Medun, troubling enough that I have decided to go spend a few days at the bedside of my dear old relative.

"Kiss me gently on the forehead, and be careful with my coiffure.

DELPHINE DE SERQUIGNY."

She inserted this missive in an envelope bearing this address:

Monsieur Baron de Hautpertuis,
in care of M. de Chaville,
Montpaillard (Nord-et-Cher)

On the second sheet of paper, she wrote, in a thoroughly French hand this time, even a bit sloppily, these words:

"My dear old rascal,

"What would you say if your little Alice showed up tomorrow at your establishment? You'd like that, wouldn't you? And besides, I owe it to you, just between us. Until tomorrow then, you old rascal. A telegram will tell you what time I'm arriving.

"Your little roast guinea hen,

ALICE."

She inserted this missive into an envelope which bore this address:

M. Bluette, Director of the Prison,
Montpaillard (Nord-et-Cher).

"Augustine!"
"Madame?"
"Mail these two letters."
"Very well, madame."

The dissatisfaction of Mlle. Delphine de Serqui-gny, or, more correctly, Mlle. Alice Cloquet, had dis-sipated, like a light cloud.

On the contrary, even, the young woman was be-side herself with joy at the idea of spending a few days in prison with her former boyfriend, one of her first, the one that she remembered most fondly and most happily. She had ruined him, it's true (Paris is so ex-pensive!), but ruined him so sweetly, and they both had so much fun, during the time that they were to-gether!

Then came the fatal separation, but as friends: he left to become director of Montpaillard Prison, she became quite fashionable, quite popular, quite Del-phine de Serquigny, but she's still a good sort, and the proof is that she remembers her little Bluette, and is filled with joy at the pleasure she will give him when she visits him.

"And besides, I owe it to him," she repeats with a little twinge of remorse, a very very little twinge...

ℭHAPTER XII

In which our excellent friend Blaireau continues to demonstrate exceptional greatness of spirit and a most accommodating character.

The morning of the day that he believes will be his last behind bars, Blaireau rises with the dawn, and his joyous song awakens all of the establishment's guests.

(It is part of the director's system to let the prisoners sing, for music not only mellows character, but probitizes it.)

In the courtyard where he goes to smoke his pipe, he meet Victor, one of the guards:

"Well, Blaireau! Up already?"

"Yes, Victor, here I am, already up! And tomorrow morning, I'll probably get up even earlier. All the same, they're not releasing me any too soon!"

"Ah! Go file a complaint then! You've never had it so good as these past three months!"

"Oh, I'm not complaining, but, say what you like,

it's not as good as freedom."

"That depends on your tastes."

"And besides, it would have been too much if they mistreated me, me an innocent man!"

"No, Blaireau, please, don't bore us with your nonsense. Innocent! I can understand you saying that when you got here, but now it's not worth the trouble."

"You'll notice, old man, that I don't insist. At the beginning, I was furious, oh yes, I was furious! But now, I don't care. I accept it. M. Bluette is a fine man, you're a great guy, the others are a swell bunch. I'm glad I met all of you... There are even times when I don't remember if I was guilty or innocent... I have to search my memory."

"What a joker!... Well, here's the boss!... He's an early bird today. Maybe because of that telegram he was just given."

In fact, M. Bluette held a telegram, which had apparently plunged him into vague confusion.

"Good morning, Blaireau, good morning, Victor. I don't think it will be too chilly today... Well, 'tis the season! Say, Victor..."

"Yes, sir?"

"Please go prepare the blue room, fix it up nicely, get it ready for someone..."

"Very well, sir."

"I'm expecting... someone... a lady... a cousin who's coming to spend a few days here... while her husband does his two weeks."

"Poor man!" said Blaireau. "There's someone who

won't find it too chilly either, if they make him do a bit of gymnastics!"

In fact, M. Bluette had forgotten, in his pious falsehood, that the Minister of Defense was not summoning citizens to boot camp at that time.

"Oh," he corrected himself, "the lady's husband won't suffer much from the heat... He's serving his two weeks as assistant director at a prison in the colonies."

"In the shade, then!" smiled Blaireau. "Good luck to him. As for me, I've had enough shade!"

"That's right, my friend, you're leaving us today... You've paid, as wise men say, your debt to society."

"Oh! My debt..."

"Victor, take our friend to the cloakroom, and give him back the clothes he had when he arrived."

"Very well, sir."

"After which, Blaireau, meet me in my office, and we'll complete the usual little formalities... I'll miss you, Blaireau."

"Me too, M. Bluette."

"And I'll remember you fondly. To begin with, you entered Montpaillard prison the same day that I did... You're leaving a bit before me..."

"I'll come see you from time to time, if you like."

"It would give me great pleasure... I like to believe that this little misadventure has been a lesson to you, and that from now on, you'll give up poaching."

"Yes, sir."

"And that you'll show more respect for authority."

"I promise you, sir."

"Beating up a constable is not dishonorable, but it is excessive."

"I won't do it anymore."

But suddenly Blaireau slammed his fist on the desk.

"What's wrong, Blaireau?" asked Bluette in astonishment. "You seem upset."

"I... I... sir, I... Damn it!... I... I'm happy to promise that I won't do it again, but I didn't do it in the first place... I don't claim, damn it, that I never poached now and then, here and there, but beating up Parju, no, I swear to you, M. Bluette, when it comes to that, I'm as innocent as a little newborn lamb!"

"Please, Blaireau, don't start in again with your foolishness! You're an excellent fellow, your flycasting is unsurpassed, and you handle a net with remarkable skill. It's too bad that such fine qualities are marred by this ridiculous obsession with claiming that you're innocent."

"But sir..."

"It's old hat, my poor Blaireau, give it up."

"Listen, M. Bluette, you've been very kind to me, I don't want to upset you. Would you like it if I said I was guilty?"

"I'd prefer it."

"Well then, I'm guilty. Are you happy now?... It's not true, but I'm guilty."

"Finally, Blaireau! You're reasonable at last!"

"And besides, whether I'm guilty or not!... Since I'm leaving today, it doesn't really matter."

"That's another way to look at it."

"So, sir, I'll go change my clothes..."

"All right... Me, I'm off to the station to meet my cousin, after which I'll set you free. Are you in a hurry?"

Blaireau winked with a supremely sly smile:

"I am in a hurry," he said, "but not as much as you, M. Bluette. I can wait until you get back with your... cousin."

"What does that mean, Blaireau?"

"Nothing, sir... If she's on the three o'clock train, your little lady, you're just in time."

"Off I go."

CHAPTER XIII

In which Montpaillard Prison appears to be an even less austere establishment than one might have supposed.

As Blaireau had said, he was just in time. The train stopped.

A pretty little woman, tousled, mischievous, not yet quite awake, jumped onto the platform, then, noticing Bluette, affected a ceremonious and haughty demeanor:

"Good morning, director sir," she said with a bow.

Then, in a whisper:

"Hello, you old rascal. I'm so happy to see you, you know, so very happy!"

"And me too!" murmured, quite sincerely, our young and amiable functionary.

"Is it far, your little club?"

"Barely a quarter of an hour."

"Let's walk then, so I can stretch my poor little

leggies."

"I don't need to remind you, Alice, that at least on the street…"

"I should behave myself. Well, see if this doesn't look like a proper old English lady."

And Alice assumed an air of respectability worthy of the vaudeville stage, which turned many heads as she passed.

Fortunately, they got there.

....

....

Those two lines of dots will discreetly replace the details of Alice's installation into the lovely blue room, an installation which the gallant M. Bluette insisted on supervising himself.

It was almost eleven o'clock when the couple went down to the directorial office.

"Have a seat, my little Alice, and be patient while I attend to my important business."

"Attend, my friend, attend."

"It will probably take about fifteen minutes."

"And that's what you call your 'important business'! It's true that, for you, it's still pretty nice… I can't believe that you're director of something."

"And yet it's the hideous truth."

"You must not be too severe with the guys."

"Severe? What for?"

"Are they wicked?"

"Not in the slightest. They're excellent fellows."

"Will you introduce me?"

"If you like. I can boast that I've made Montpail-lard Prison into a veritable family prison. Everyone lives here in harmony and tranquility."

"All the better, little rascal."

"The only thing is that life here can be a little monotonous. We don't have much amusement except the arrival or release of a prisoner from time to time. In fact, there's one who just finished his sentence today, who I have to set free. I mustn't forget about him, which has happened to me on several occasions."

"Who is it?"

"A certain Blaireau, an expert poacher, a very friendly chap besides. You'll see."

"Did he commit a crime?"

"Oh no, the poor lad! A little mishap, nothing at all, he just assaulted a constable."

"Isn't that allowed?"

"Of course, but you shouldn't get caught."

At that moment, one of the guards brought the director's mail, which the latter set carelessly on his desk.

"Nothing new, except for that?"

"No, sir... Ah!" the guard remarked. "Do you remember that Blaireau is to be released today?"

"Yes... yes... I told him... In fact, please send him to me now, and I'll wrap up this business."

"I'll send Blaireau, sir," said the guard as he left.

Bluette turned to his young friend:

"Be good enough to leave me for a moment,

my little Alice. I'll send my man on his way, and then we'll have the whole day to ourselves."

CHAPTER XIV

In which Blaireau feels all of his philosophy abandon him.

"Knock knock knock!"

"Come in!" cried Bluette.

And as Blaireau made his appearance, his long arms swinging at his sides, fingers spread, a smile on his face, the director tried to assume an administrative attitude. He sat at his desk, toyed with a letter opener, coughed a bit.

"Approach, Blaireau."

"Here I am, sir, here I am."

Blaireau stood before Bluette, seeming to question him with his eyes, as if asking, "Now then! Am I free? Or am I not?"

Bluette leaned on his elbows, with a benevolent look at his guest. Then, with a certain firmness, he began:

"Blaireau," he said, "in a quarter of an hour you will be free. We just have to sign these papers, and all doors will open before you. You were sentenced to three months of detention, you have served three months and a day, you have done your time."

"What!" said Blaireau, lifting up his nose. "I did an extra day?"

"Of course," the director calmly replied.

"Why?"

"You ask me why, Blaireau?"

"Damn!"

Bluette thought for a moment, and, not coming up with an explanation that seemed plausible, contented himself with saying:

"It's an old administrative custom."

"It's a funny one, your old administrative custom," said Blaireau, with a gentle laugh... "Bah," he added philosophically, "maybe it's because of leap year."

"Probably," said Bluette, who had never bothered to form an opinion on the subject.

He handed a register to Blaireau:

"Sign there... and there..."

Blaireau took the pen clumsily, and slowly began to trace the letters of his name, not without some suspicion.

From time to time, he looked at Bluette, as if to assure himself that the latter was not trying to trick him. But the director wore his kindest expression, and his eyes were nothing but sympathetic.

"Eh, Blaireau! Do you know that you have beautiful

handwriting?"

"You're too kind, sir."

And he scrawled a magnificent flourish on the blank page.

"There! That's it, I'm free."

Bluette then arose, walked over to the poacher, and held out a friendly hand. Blaireau, quite moved, extended his.

"Goodbye, my friend, and stay in touch... now and then."

"Certainly!" cried Blaireau. "I won't forget your kindness, sir, and if you like wild game..."

"I like it very much."

"Very well! I'll send you some, one of these days, that won't set you back much."

And Blaireau added, as a sort of afterthought:

"Nor me, for that matter."

"And so you'll continue your poaching?" said Bluette with a tinge of reproach.

"Damn! Not everyone can be a functionary, sir."

"Obviously not, my friend, obviously not. Follow that profession then, since it's yours, but follow it in moderation."

"I promise."

"Without violence?"

"I am a gentle soul."

"And try to reconcile the demands of your profession with the respect that a good citizen owes to authority."

"I'll do my best."

"And so, Blaireau, from now on, no more attacks on constables?"

"He insists on it, don't contradict him," thought Blaireau. And he added, in a conciliatory tone:

"I swear to it, sir, but only to please you. Goodbye, M. Bluette."

"Goodbye, Blaireau."

During this brief conversation, Bluette had begun automatically to open his mail, and the first letter that caught his attention was one bearing the stamp of the public prosecutor.

He deciphered the first few lines just as Blaireau, having respectfully made his farewell several times, put his hand on the doorknob and prepared to leave.

"Oh, my God!" the director suddenly cried.

"What is it?" murmured Blaireau, turning around.

"Imagine that! It's fantastic!" continued Bluette, leaning over the letter to read it more carefully.

"I'm going, sir, I'm going," said Blaireau, moving off discreetly.

Bluette raised his eyes.

"Good heavens, no! Don't leave."

"Why shouldn't I leave?"

"I have to talk to you... Come here..."

And as Blaireau crossed the directorial office with his shuffling step, Bluette read and reread:

"The guilty party has made a complete confession and turned himself in to the authorities."

He passed his hand over his forehead and looked at Blaireau. And so, Blaireau was not mistaken, when he claimed that he was innocent! And so, we are in the presence of a miscarriage of justice! Yes, it was fantastic! Absolutely fantastic. He would look back on it in his old age, an interesting chapter for his future memoirs as a prison director. "When I tell Alice," thought Bluette, "won't she be content."

A miscarriage of justice, there's a good thing to break up the monotony of an administrative career!

Blaireau, standing before the desk, waited in silence, respecting the thoughts that visibly preoccupied Bluette.

Then, the latter, looking deep into the poacher's eyes, asked him:

"What would you say, Blaireau, if I told you that you're innocent?"

Our man was startled.

"Me!"

"Yes, you..."

Blaireau quickly recovered and replied:

"Well, sir, I would say that I already knew that."

"You're innocent, Blaireau; you're right, you're absolutely right..."

And Bluette, who still could not believe it, repeated the terms of the official letter:

"A complete confession. The innocence of the aforementioned Blaireau is established. After the indispensable formalities, he will be released as soon as possible..."

"My God!" said Blaireau. "I was sure that I was innocent, but I'm pleased to hear it anyway. It makes me feel even more sure. And," he added, "the guilty party, if you don't mind my asking, who is he?"

"A teacher, apparently."

"A teacher!" cried Blaireau, raising his arms... "Ah well, if the teachers are joining in, now!"

"A certain Fléchard (Jules). You shouldn't hold it against him, Blaireau."

"I don't hold it against him... but he could have turned himself in earlier. Just at the moment when I'm done!... It hardly seems worth it, so to speak."

"There are many in his place," Bluette remarked judiciously, "who wouldn't have turned themselves in at all."

"Still!" muttered Blaireau.

The director continued:

"Nevertheless, my friend, I'm very happy for you that it ended like this."

He held out his hand again to Blaireau, then, crinkling the letter:

"The public prosecutor will act promptly. And for my part, I shall spare no effort, and you'll be freed as soon as possible."

"What did you say?"

Bluette repeated:

"As soon as possible, I promise you."

Blaireau's shoulders shook with a peal of boyish laughter:

"But, sir, aren't you forgetting something?"

"And what's that, my dear Blaireau?"

"You forgot that you just freed me, and that I'm

leaving now."

"No, not right away," Bluette coolly replied.

"Eh?"

"Yes," continued the director, resuming his usual benevolent expression. "The letter from the public prosecutor said 'as soon as possible.'"

"And?"

"And I can't take it upon myself to release you immediately."

Blaireau made a great effort to understand.

"But I finished my sentence!"

The director did not seem swayed by this argument, however reasonable it might seem at first blush. He smiled indulgently.

"You served your sentence as a guilty man, my dear Blaireau. But today I'm told, out of the blue, that you're innocent. The situation therefore has changed, and we find ourselves with new formalities that must be attended to."

Blaireau's eyes began to widen in anger:

"So, if I wanted to leave now, I couldn't?"

"No, my friend."

"You'd stop me?"

"Without violence, my dear Blaireau, but I'd stop you all the same."

"And yet I was free just now?"

"You were, Blaireau,"

"And now I'm not?"

"Well, at least not immediately."

Blaireau erupted:

"So that's how it is, damn it all! Because I'm innocent, now I have to stay in prison a little longer?"

"That's not the only reason," the director ironically replied.

Forgetting his customary politeness, Blaireau began to pace through the office, shaking his head and emitting exclamations of rage.

"This is too much! It's too much!... No..."

"Come now! Calm yourself, my friend," said Bluette, laying a friendly hand on his shoulder. "All is not lost..."

"This is the last straw."

"As soon as possible, I'll go to the public prosecutor, I'll explain your situation, and one of these days, I hope..."

"One of these days!" cried Blaireau.

"Tomorrow perhaps..."

"Oh!"

"Or, who knows... Maybe even this evening."

Blaireau dropped into a chair, not without a hint of discouragement.

"You must admit, M. Bluette, that this is..."

"Good lord, my dear Blaireau, have a little patience! The law is the law. To go to prison, it's not always essential to be guilty; on the other hand, to be freed, it's not always enough to be innocent!"

"It's not that I regret," Blaireau politely remarked, "spending a few more hours with you..."

"You're too kind..."

"But what a bizarre idea he had to turn himself in,

that teacher!"

"Indeed."

"Everything was going so well!"

"Don't worry, my friend. We'll eventually set you free anyway."

"I certainly hope so!"

And they both began to laugh, together, with no concern for the social chasm that lay between them.

Blaireau suddenly had a practical idea:

"Couldn't I ask for damages?"

"I wouldn't advise it," Bluette replied.

A man entered.

"Someone wishes to speak with the director immediately; here's his card."

Bluette read: André Guilloche, attorney-at-law (for the Blaireau affair).

"Ho ho," said Bluette, "here's a lawyer who's interested in you."

Blaireau was instinctively suspicious.

"And now, what's this? A lawyer for the Blaireau affair! What? Sentenced to three months in prison for a crime he didn't commit, ready to leave today, his time served to the last second. And now he's kept in prison! And now a lawyer wants to talk to him! What will happen to him next... Ah, woe is me! This is what they call justice."

Chapter XV

In which Blaireau sees the dawn breaking — a fair return for the vicissitudes of life — upon a glorious situation for him.

M. Guilloche, a thick portfolio under his arm, rushed in like the wind, delighted with the turn that things had taken.

"My dear Bluette, you know what brings me here; I come to ask you to put me in contact, if the internal regulations of your prison permit it, of course, with the unfortunate victim of this sorry affair."

Bluette burst out laughing.

"The unfortunate victim of this sorry affair is right here."

Blaireau felt reassured at the lawyer's words. He obviously hadn't come to cause him trouble, this lawyer, because he was sorry for him, because he called him an unfortunate victim. Ha! Maybe, on the contrary, there was a windfall coming... Maybe there was a way to get something from the situation. In any case, it wouldn't hurt to exaggerate things a bit.

And so he assumed his most miserable expression to answer M. Guilloche:

"Yes, sir, I'm the poor unfortunate victim."

And he added with a heavy sigh:

"Ah, how I've suffered!"

"I don't doubt it, my poor friend, but your torment will soon be at an end."

"And none too soon."

"I just went to the public prosecutor's office, I received a copy of your records, I moved heaven and earth..."

"Oh, thank you, sir, thank you!"

"You'll be set free this very day... Ah, they didn't seem too happy at the public prosecutor's office!"

"They looked kind of bothered, eh?"

"Very bothered!... This adventure is bound to cause quite a stir. Did you read my article in the *Nord-et-Cher Clarion*?"

"No sir, here in prison we only read the *Little Paper*."

"I brought you a copy, so you could peruse it."

Blaireau seized the gazette, and read these words, printed in gigantic letters:

A SCANDAL IN MONTPAILLARD
THE BLAIREAU AFFAIR
SERIOUS MISCARRIAGE OF JUSTICE

"I hadn't realized it at first," he murmured, "but it's true, it's a miscarriage of justice. I'm the victim of a miscarriage of justice."

And he repeated to himself, with the pride that any growing notoriety brings:

"The Blaireau affair! The Blaireau affair! Now I have an affair named after me!"

"Read, my friend."

Blaireau read:

"The unhappy victim, whom one of the most serious miscarriages of justice committed by the courts in the last quarter century has left for years in Montpaillard Prison..."

"Oh, for years!" Blaireau protested mildly. "That's a bit of an exaggeration."

"We'll correct it in one of the next issues."

"The length of time isn't really important," Blaireau affirmed. "I'll continue."

"...for years in Montpaillard Prison, the unfortunate Blaireau will be avenged by public opinion. As for us, we shall not abandon him!

Signed, THE EDITOR."

Blaireau became prouder and prouder:

"Sir, please thank the editor for me, and tell him that he's not dealing with an ungrateful man. If he ever needs a fine rabbit, or a handsome trout..."

"He thanks you, Blaireau."

"Oh, as far as newspaper articles go, that's what I call a newspaper article! I wish I could write one like that!"

"You do better than write them, my dear comrade,

you inspire them!"

And he grasped his hand warmly.

"But that's not all, Blaireau."

"What else is there?"

"Think for a moment. Let the idea sink in that you are no longer the simple and banal Blaireau that you were before."

"I'm letting it sink in, sir; but how am I not the simple and banal Blaireau that I was before?"

"By the fact that today the world has its gaze turned upon you."

"Damn!"

"Your name is no longer yours alone: it is now that of a public scandal."

"That's absolutely true."

"And thus you are quite naturally seen as the standard bearer for the persecuted."

"That's what I'll be!"

"Don't forget that this position creates certain duties that you must not shirk."

"Don't worry, sir. If you knew me better, you'd know that I'm not the type to shirk my duties. The standard bearer for the persecuted, yes, that's what I'll be! Yes!" he repeated forcefully.

"Bravo, Blaireau! In your breast beats the heart of the citizens of yesteryear!"

"Huh! Who would have thought, a year ago, that I'd become a standard bearer!"

"To begin with, my old comrade, you will dine, this evening, with the entire staff of the Clarion."

"I accept."

Here, the director thought it necessary to add a timid observation:

"My dear sir, I don't know if the internal regulations of the prison really permit me to let prisoners accept dinner invitations in town. But given the unusual circumstances..."

"Oh, yes!" Blaireau bitterly cried. "*Unusual*, you can certainly call them unusual, these circumstances!"

"In a little while, then, I'll come to get you, my dear Blaireau, and soon, when it's time for the elections, you'll be the honorary president at all our meetings."

"Honorary president! I'd like that, but would I know how?"

"Nothing could be simpler. I'll teach you."

"I'll preside with my standard?"

"What standard?"

"The standard for the persecuted, of course!"

"Ha ha ha! The standard for the persecuted, my friend, doesn't really exist. It's an expression... a figure of speech."

"It doesn't matter. I'll carry myself as if I had one."

"That's it... Speaking of which, you'll probably receive a visit from Mayor Dubenoît. He'll try to make trouble for you... Be careful. In fact, here he is!"

$\mathcal{C}$HAPTER $\mathcal{XVI}$

In which there is a renewal of the conflict between M. André Guilloche, attorney-at-law in Montpaillard, and M. Dubenoît, mayor of said community.

M. Dubenoît was indeed approaching, and upon his features could be read simultaneously anxiety, discontent, and a number of other disagreeable emotions.

"Good day, my dear Bluette! Ah, here's the formidable Blaireau, the hero of the day! He's the one I want to talk to, but he's in deep conversation, I see, with our young revolutionary."

"Blaireau," said Guilloche, "has decided to choose me as his lawyer."

"Say rather that you chose Blaireau as a client."

"It's the same thing," Blaireau said, in reconciliation.

"I read your article this morning, my dear Guilloche. It's charming... and in such good faith!"

"Did you really think, Your Honor, that it could happen like that! That an innocent man could be imprisoned for years!"

"Three months, if you please."

"And that public opinion would not protest!"

"Public opinion doesn't care a fig for Blaireau."

"Governments have been overthrown for less, Your Honor!"

"Those times are over, counselor!"

"Perhaps not as much as you think... Will you do me the honor, M. Dubenoît, of attending a talk that I'm giving tomorrow at the Future Tavern?"

"On what subject?"

"Miscarriages of justice in France, from Saint Louis under the oak until today."

"I can't promise to attend in person, but, in any case, I'll send a boy from City Hall."

"You're too kind."

And he thought, "The mayor is furious!"

"Goodbye, gentlemen! I'll see you soon, Blaireau, and don't forget your promises."

"Don't worry, sir, I'm a straight-ahead guy, as they say."

$\mathcal{C}$HAPTER $\mathcal{X}$VII

In which we see that an overly exclusive love for order can goad a public functionary into formal iniquity.

"Just the two of us, Blaireau."

"I'm listening, Your Honor."

"So, you damn fool, you'd let yourself be shanghaied by a bunch of conspirators who'll use you to irritate authority and the courts, to trouble law and order, and, after this fine mess, toss you aside as they laugh at you!"

"Why would they laugh at me?"

"Because they won't need you anymore, damn it all! It's obvious!... Listen, Blaireau, you have to examine your situation calmly."

"It's not too cheerful, my situation."

"Not too cheerful? I don't suppose you're going to complain about the food in prison, eh? Montpaillard Prison is well known as the best in the department, and you won't always come across directors like M. Bluette."

"I hope I never come across any other directors."

"You never know."

"And besides, M. Bluette is very nice, but still, a prison is always a prison."

"When you go to another one, you'll appreciate the difference."

"And so, you're set on this idea, that I go back to prison?"

"Let's drop the subject. Let's throw a veil over the past. How do you plan to earn a living now?"

"I'll have no trouble."

"Really? And what will you do?"

"I'll work."

"At what?"

"Like before... as... a handyman."

"A handyman? I know what that means, but we'll keep an eye on you, my boy, and now more than ever. Do you think it will be easy to find steady work?"

"Why not?"

"That's where you're mistaken, my poor friend. People will know that you served three months in prison. They won't like that very much!"

"But, for heaven's sake, they'll also know that I'm innocent!"

"I know that, Blaireau, and I'm not talking about myself, I'm above such prejudices. I would gladly welcome, I who speak to you now, an innocent man to my table, but you won't find the same indulgence in everyone, will you, Blaireau?"

"Alas, it's true!"

"You must consider public opinion."

"Public opinion?" cried Blaireau. "It's in my favor, public opinion. Here, take a look at this paper."

"Ah, you read that nonsense!"

"'A scandal in Montpaillard!'"

"There is no scandal in Montpaillard, and there never will be! I'll show them!"

"And 'the Blaireau affair,' Your Honor, what will you do about that?

"There is no Blaireau affair! The very idea! Do you imagine, my poor boy, that just because the *Nord-et-Cher Clarion* printed your name in big letters, you've become a more important person than you were three months ago, before you were convicted?"

"I'm sure of it!"

"You're mistaken, my dear Blaireau. Before you were convicted, you weren't guilty... Today, you're innocent. It's exactly the same thing, and your situation has not changed one iota."

"I don't agree. And besides, I spent three months in prison during that time. Let's not forget that little detail..."

"Come now, just between us, right? Don't try to get cute with me. You served three months in prison, it's true; but if you added up all the months of prison that you deserve for your poaching crimes alone, it's not three months of prison that you'd deserve, my friend, but at least ten years. Consider yourself lucky, then, and let's drop the subject!"

"I'm innocent, and I won't forget it!"

"My word, you seem to think you're the only innocent man in the commune! Do you know what I think, Blaireau? You're a bad apple, an agent of disorder, that's what you are!"

"It doesn't change the fact that I'm innocent."

"Listen, Blaireau, I'll give you one final word of advice, advice from a friend. Go away from here. Go to some faraway place in the country, some place that I'll even find for you. There, through hard work and good conduct, perhaps some day you can rehabilitate yourself."

"What do you mean, rehabilitate myself? Me, an innocent man?"

"Are we agreed?"

"Never! An innocent man doesn't need rehabilitation!"

"If you ignore my advice, Blaireau, you can't blame me for what will happen."

"What will happen?"

"You'll see, and it might even be too late, you stubborn fool!"

"Damn, damn, now I'm all confused."

Blaireau scratched his poor puzzled head. A guard announced the arrival of a gentleman who sought permission from the director to visit M. Blaireau.

This gentleman was none other than our old acquaintance the Baron de Hautpertuis, who came to see the unhappy victim, and to discuss with him the details of the gala organized in his honor and for his benefit.

"A baron," said Blaireau. "Wow!"

"Show the gentleman in," ordered the director.

"Hasn't he given up on that ridiculous idea?" grumbled Dubenoît. "Because there aren't enough revolutionaries, now the nobility has to get involved, in disturbing the peace. What strange times, my God, what strange times!"

In a sober yet elegant outfit, with no flower in his buttonhole (flowers are not worn when visiting prisoners), the Baron de Hautpertuis introduced himself, in a relaxed yet serious manner, as befitted the circumstances.

$\mathscr{C}$HAPTER $\mathscr{XVIII}$

In which Blaireau's situation, already glorious, is revealed, which
makes nothing worse, as ever more remunerative.

In a few words, Blaireau was caught up to date.

Assisted by the brilliant youth of Montpaillard, the Baron de Hautpertuis was organizing a splendid gala for the benefit of the unfortunate Blaireau, a gala which would be the event of the season.

"A gala for me!"

"Yes, a gala for you, my dear... what was your name again?"

"Blaireau... My name is Blaireau. You know: the Blaireau affair!"

"Of course, now I remember. Yes, M. Blaireau, even now we're organizing something truly marvelous, a splendid gala in which you will be the hero!"

"The hero! I'll be the hero!"

Blaireau stood proudly: only a quarter of an hour

ago, he was promoted to standard bearer of the persecuted, and now he'd become a hero! Hero of a gala organized by a baron!

Well, things were certainly turning out nicely!

After glory, money!

M. Dubenoît, on the other hand, became sadder and sadder at seeing law and order in Montpaillard decidedly compromised.

He made one last attempt:

"Don't you think, Baron, that a good position as gardener would be more suitable for this young man?"

Blaireau grimaced:

"Bah! A good position as gardener. They're pretty rare, you know, good positions as gardeners."

"And besides," added the Baron, "there will be time to find a position for him after the gala, when this unfortunate lad will have received the proceeds from this fine manifestation of public charity."

Blaireau's eyes opened wide, and his ears no less so:

"I'll receive the proceeds, Baron, sir? I'll receive... all of it?"

"Yes, my friend, you'll receive it all, minus a few insignificant expenses, and a few small costs for the gala."

"Of course... And how much do you think it will come to, the profit, approximately?"

"Oh," laughed the mayor, "how much do you think it will come to?"

"Good Lord, I really have no idea."

"Well then! My dear Baron, let me tell you that a gala like that won't take in twenty francs, here in Montpaillard."

"Twenty francs? You're joking!"

"Montpaillard is not a wealthy city, Baron."

"Just yesterday you were saying that there are no poor people in the district?"

"There are no poor people, it's true, but no rich ones either. Montpaillard, Baron, is composed of people who are comfortable (*more animated*), tranquil! (*pacing angrily*) peaceful! (*gesticulating*). People who violently reject the Parisian innovations with which the capital hopes to poison the provinces, no offense intended, my dear Baron!"

"I'm not offended, Your Honor, I'm simply surprised."

"Well, I'll bet you five hundred francs that your gala won't make two hundred francs."

"I accept. That's twenty-five louis more for Blaireau's coffer. Blaireau, you can thank M. Dubenoît."

"This is the first time," said Blaireau, "that His Honor has ever been nice to me. Thank you, Your Honor!"

"You're quite welcome, my boy, you'll see, because this famous gala will be an enormous fiasco."

M. de Hauterpertuis was cut to the quick.

"My dear M. Dubenoît, in my life I've organized seventy-one charity galas following a variety of catastrophes. I've saved from disaster Peruvians, Turks, Portuguese, Chinese, Moldavians, Egyptians...

It would be funny if I didn't succeed, the first time that I organize a gala for the benefit of a compatriot."

"If you knew Montpaillard, you wouldn't talk like that."

"I take full responsibility!"

"We'll talk again... Gentlemen, I must leave you, I'm expected at City Hall."

It was time for M. Dubenoît to leave; he was about to explode.

CHAPTER XIX

"Your prison, sir, is far more cheerful than I'd have imagined. A superb view, a lovely garden... Have you been here long?"

"Three months, exactly three months. I arrived the same day as our excellent Blaireau. That's why I feel such affection for him."

"I can understand that. And before Montpaillard..."

"I began my career with this establishment. Before that, I lived in Paris. Ah! If someone had told me, only three years ago, that I'd become director of a prison, I'd have laughed."

"You'd planned, I assume, to pursue some other line of work?"

"I planned nothing at all... I just had a good time. My word, I regret nothing, because, really, I had a very good time indeed."

"Say no more! And women, I suppose?"

"Yes, women, one especially!"

"Splendid!"

"Yes, a woman is responsible for my entry into this administrative career. Her name was Alice. We adored one another... The man that you see before you, Baron, was a simple man of independent means. Alice soon put a stop to that abnormal situation. She threw money out the window, and I watched it fall..."

"That's very jolly. Ruined by women! Let me shake your hand."

"Not by women, by one woman."

"That's even more flattering."

"So, utterly ruined, I sought a place in the government. At the time, I had a cousin, a minister of state..."

"Is he no longer your cousin?"

"He's no longer a minister. He had just enough time to appoint me to Montpaillard. It was lucky for me, for the state of my finances permitted me either to become a prisoner myself, or a prison director. I didn't hesitate a second."

"I can well believe it. And Mlle. Alice?"

"Alice, for her part, met an elderly and wealthy gentleman; but the dear little thing hasn't forgotten me, I know that now for sure."

"Congratulations, my dear Bluette! I didn't expect to find a prison director who was such a charming fellow, and I'm enchanted to have met you."

"The pleasure is all mine. Will you do me the honor

of visiting my little establishment? Of course, it's not Fresnes Prison!"

"I'd be delighted, dear sir."

The few words exchanged about Alice had stirred in Bluette's heart sudden remorse at leaving the sweet little thing in such prolonged solitude.

"Before we begin our tour, Baron, I must beg your permission to attend to a few administrative details."

"Go, my dear director, go! Duty comes first!"

And Bluette ran off to rejoin Alice, whom he embraced with all his heart, even, I believe we can affirm, several times.

CHAPTER XX

In which Blaireau dons the unwholesome livery of popularity.

M. Bluette had no sooner turned on his heels than M. Guilloche made a new and sudden appearance.

"Good day, Baron. You're doing well?"

"Quite well, as are you, I imagine, for, judging by the thickness of your portfolio, the chicanery business must be booming."

The fact is that the portfolio that M. Guilloche carried under his arm seemed crammed to the point of bursting.

"Tell me, Baron, will M. Bluette be gone long?"

"For a few moments, I believe. He's off giving a few orders, he told me."

"So, there's no time to lose. Blaireau, I brought you some clothes."

"Some good clothes?"

"Magnificent clothes."

"Ah, so much the better! There's nothing I like as much as good clothes! If I had the money, nobody in the country would dress as well as me!"

"Well then, here are your clothes!"

Guilloche extracted from his portfolio a complete suit, whose appearance brought immediate cries of horror from M. de Hautpertuis and howls of indignation from Blaireau.

A suit which would discourage both the pencil of Callot and the palette of Goya!

Formless rags, tatters of no definable color, with holes, with tears, a hideous and grim polychromy of stitching and patches.

At first suffocated to the point of apoplexy, Blaireau then thought it was a joke, an excellent joke by his lawyer.

"That's a good one, M. Guilloche!"

"Come on, Blaireau! Quickly! We have no time to lose!"

"You want me to put that on?"

"Of course!"

So it was serious then! Blaireau didn't understand:

"You're making fun of me, aren't you?"

"I'm not making fun of you, Blaireau. This is the suit that you'll wear for your release from prison."

"You call that a suit? Well, don't worry! I'd never be seen in the street with rags like that on my back! An innocent man! What would people think of me?"

"But you must, you must. There will be more than

five hundred people waiting at the prison door for your release... You'll cause a sensation, I promise."

"I can believe it, with that pile of scraps. No, I won't do it!"

"But you don't understand, innocent child that you are, that the shabbier you are, the more the public will pity you! Just ask M. de Hautpertuis."

"It's obvious," agreed the Baron.

"And so," Blaireau cried, "you, Baron, would consent to wear this?"

"In the habitual circumstances of life, my friend, no! But in the current situation, I wouldn't hesitate a second. When the crowd sees you, they're sure to cheer!"

"And even carry you in triumph," agreed Guilloche. "Besides, the demonstration is very well organized. The party members are rehearsing it now."

The promise of an upcoming triumph decided Blaireau.

"All right, give me your castoffs!"

With a flick of the wrist, he removed his own clothes and put on the sordid rags.

A cry of admiration came from Guilloche.

"Honestly, Blaireau, you're superb!"

The Baron adjusted his monocle:

"Brilliant, my friend, very chic! At the famous rag-tag ball that the duchess gave, last winter, I don't remember seeing such picturesque tatters."

"All the same, Baron, I'd rather have a suit more like yours."

"I'll give you the address of my tailor."

"When I get the money from the gala..."

He was interrupted by a burst of laughter. It was Bluette, who suddenly came across the masquerade:

"What's all this? My poor Blaireau, you look terrible!"

"It was I," explained Guilloche, "who took it upon myself to bring my client a few things, since he had nothing suitable to wear. And so..."

"I won't hide the fact, my dear sir, that the internal regulations of the prison do not authorize me to allow my prisoners to wear such a costume, even in Carnival season."

"I thought that under the present circumstances, I could somehow..."

Blaireau now considered himself thoroughly chic, as the Baron had said, and the prospect of his upcoming triumph excited him to the point of losing his usual reserve.

He had now fully assumed his role:

"Well, that's the last straw, I must say!" he cried. "After having suffered all that I've suffered, now I don't even have the right to dress as I please! This is too much!"

$\mathcal{C}$HAPTER $\sim$ XXL

In which the Baron de Hautpertuis does all that he can to deserve the word at the end.

When Bluette planted, temporarily of course, a final kiss on the nape of Alice's neck, as he said, "I'll be all yours in a few minutes, at this moment my office is full of visitors," he committed the serious error of not specifying the names and descriptions of the inopportune callers.

If he had, he could have avoided, not a tragedy, for the adventure turned out better than one might have expected, but a dangerous complication.

On hearing the name of the Baron de Hautpertuis, Alice, or, if you prefer, Delphine de Serquigny, would have leapt to her feet, as in the melodramas:

"That man here!"

The Baron's name had never been pronounced between Alice and Bluette. Why talk about such matters?

And when Bluette, recounting his life to the Baron, mentioned his adorable Alice, M. de Hautpertuis was a hundred miles away from believing that the charming woman constituted the same person as his own beloved Delphine.

And thus does life arrange its surprises and its encounters, all much more ingenious than those imagined by our darkling playwrights, or our most farcical vaudevillians, as the critic says.

Left alone, the merry Alice was bored stiff, and, as idleness is a poor counselor, our young friend did not hesitate to commit one of those acts which the most indulgent censors are unanimous in qualifying as anti-administrative.

Discovering in a storeroom a supply of clothing intended for prisoners, she chose one that was approximately her size, and put it on.

As much as to make herself comfortable (chinos are so cool in the summer!) as to surprise Bluette when he saw her dressed like that.

Let us add that our little comrade looked very nice indeed in this usually hideous uniform, so true is it that youth and grace suffice to embellish, not only all that they adorn, but all that adorns them!

....

After having fully savored this delicate and thoroughly original observation, let us return to the center of the action.

Since it was very hot, Alice found nothing better to do than to look for the coolest cell in the prison, install herself, and read the Parisian paper which the mailman had just delivered.

She is quite comfortable in this light outfit which she is not afraid to get dirty; her hair is undone, and tucked into a canvas cap.

One might mistake her for some poor young man, guilty no doubt, but so appealing that the court should have acquitted him.

With a sweet little face like that, and those big expressive eyes, he must not be a very fearsome criminal! Poor little prisoner!

Meanwhile, Bluette showed the Baron around his establishment.

They had visited the cells, the workrooms, the refectory.

"Over here are the cells where we lock up the most dangerous criminals, temporarily entrusted to our care, or the difficult prisoners. These cells, since I became director, have remained empty. If you'd like to take a look..."

And as the reader might have guessed, it was none other than the cell containing Alice to which Bluette opened the door.

Here, a truly dramatic scene, which is easy to imagine.

Thanks to his severe myopia, the Baron did not notice the desperate grimaces which Alice directed to Bluette, and which the latter, fortunately, understood.

There was no doubt, my friend, Alice's lord and master was indeed he, the Baron de Hautpertuis.

Thorny, oh how thorny, was the situation! Bluette tried to lead the Baron away, but in vain, the Baron adjusted his monocle and murmured:

"This is the most startling resemblance I've ever seen in my life!"

All right, that was it! He would recognize her, and then what? How could he explain this?... Bluette was a bit worried!

As for Alice, she had not lost her nerve for an instant.

"What a startling resemblance!" repeated the Baron. "Who is this young man, my dear Bluette?"

"He's a lad who was just convicted of vagrancy, an excellent subject, apart from that."

"Do you have any family, my friend, a mother and father?"

Alice remembered that she had been an actress, in the past.

She assumed a humble expression, and gave her voice the gravelly tones of people on the lower rungs of society.

"Alas, yes, kind sir!" she replied. "I have a family, a fine family to whom I've brought nothing but despair! My poor sister, especially..."

"Ah, you have a sister, my friend? How old is she?"

"Twenty-three, sir."

"Ah! My God!"

"What's wrong, Baron?" asked Bluette.

"The same age as Delphine!" thought Hautpertuis.

"Where does she live?" he continued, addressing

the young prisoner.

"In Paris, sir. I must admit that I've caused her no end of trouble, my poor sister!"

"Her name?"

"Delphine, sir."

"My premonition was not mistaken! Oh, this is terrible! My dear M. Bluette, this poor boy is the brother of Delphine, the brother of my girlfriend."

"A strange encounter, Baron! Ah, no one would suspect all of the dramas that occur in prison!"

"Go on, my friend. Tell me about your life. Why are you here?"

"The director there told you, sir, for vagrancy. All my life, I've been nothing but a vagrant. It's stronger than I am, I must be a vagrant. In vain does my sister send me money, I spend it all as soon as I get it. Ah! I have to admit I've cost her a lot."

"Your sister sends you money!"

"Not only to me, sir, but to the whole family, to two or three brothers that we have in the south, to her old invalid uncle, to a sick aunt..."

"That's where she is now, with that sick aunt. Poor Delphine, what a kind heart! What a fine, fine girl!"

"She supports the whole family, sir. Without her, we'd have all starved to death long ago. But then, she might not always be able to send us money, and then..."

M. de Hautpertuis made a fine gesture.

"Don't worry, my young friend, your sister will never want for money, I can assure you!"

"Do you know her then, sir?"

"I have that honor."

"Poor Delphine! Without us, she could have been a respectable girl... She wouldn't have turned out so badly."

"But my friend, you mustn't believe that your sister turned out badly, that would be a terrible mistake. She's not exactly married, but she does have a friend who is sincere, devoted, wealthy, and will never let her want for anything, neither her, nor her family."

"She deserves it."

"As for you, my young friend, take this for now."

He slipped a hundred franc note in her hand.

"Thank you, sir, you're too kind."

"Just to oblige me, the director would be happy to treat you with indulgence, wouldn't you, M. Bluette?"

"I'll treat him very well," the functionary modestly replied.

"Goodbye, my dear director. Ah, this meeting has saddened my heart!"

"Life is full of strange things."

"And you, my young friend, best of luck!"

"I'm not complaining... The director is very good to me."

When she was alone, Alice could not help murmuring:

"He's a fine man, really — but what a sucker!"

CHAPTER XXII

In which several things happen, none imbued with a character of exceptional importance.

Bluette insisted on accompanying the Baron to the big door that gives onto the street.

They congratulated each other mutually on having made their charming acquaintance, and were taking their leave, when a middle aged man, an officer of the Legion of Honor, introduced himself, with an expression that was both friendly and slightly acerbic.

"M. Bluette, I assume?"

"Himself, sir."

"I am M. Devois, prison inspector."

"Ah, of course, sir. Delighted to meet you."

"I knew your predecessor quite well... I'm happy to find myself in contact with you."

"I too, sir."

"I was told, in high places, that you're a man of

great distinction, and frankly too good for the position that you now hold."

"They were only too flattering to me, in those high places."

"It even appears that you've transformed your prison into a sort of little paradise, something like a comfortable family inn."

"I do my best."

"In this case, best is the enemy of good. A prison, my dear M. Bluette, is not a casino."

"I'm well aware of that!"

"And, without violating the laws of humanity, one must be stern with the convicted, whose numbers would swell considerably if they were treated everywhere as they are in Montpaillard Prison, that is to say, as first class passengers."

"Poor prisoners!"

"By the way, what is this business about a miscarriage of justice, which I heard about this morning at the sub-prefecture?"

"It's true, sir. One of my prisoners was unjustly convicted. The guilty party turned himself in yesterday, and made a complete confession."

"That's curious."

"I'm waiting for the order from the public prosecutor to set my man free."

And our friend Bluette, whom the inspector's sarcasm inspired rather than intimidated, added in an exaggeratedly modest tone:

"I will even permit myself to call the inspector's

attention to the fact that, despite certain small irregularities which I am the first to deplore, Montpaillard Prison nevertheless contains an innocent man."

"And I congratulate you."

"There are many better run prisons that could not say as much."

"It's certainly a mark in your favor."

As they chatted, the two men arrived at the cell in which young Alice, as she read her gazettes, hummed a rather sprightly tune.

At that moment, our friend Bluette, thinking of his possible promotion, felt himself overcome by a sense of foreboding.

He coughed with uncommon violence, and with a persistence worthy of a better occasion.

Too late, alas! The inspector had opened the door to the cell.

"Well," he said, "I was not misled in high places; your establishment, M. Bluette, is a cheerful one. Who is this young prisoner, this pretty blackbird who sings in his cell?"

This time, Bluette is taken by surprise:

"This young prisoner? He's... What's his name again?..."

"This is too much, you have forty-three unfortunate prisoners, and you don't recognize them?"

"Yes, inspector, sir, I do know him, but I forgot his name. Besides, it's not important."

"Why isn't it important?"

"Because this boy is innocent. This is the innocent

man we were just talking about."

"What a strange prison! You have an innocent man, and you lock him in a cell!... It's true that the poor boy doesn't seem too upset by it. Come out, my friend, this is no place for you."

Victor, the guard, brings Bluette a card:

"This gentleman insists on seeing you immediately."

"'Jules Fléchard, instructor of gymnastics'; tell him to come back later."

"Why?" says the inspector. "Go receive the gentleman. I'll continue my tour alone while I wait."

Bluette obeys, but with what anxiety in his heart!

"My God! My God! What will happen next?" he says, trembling. "My administrative career seems to be singularly compromised!"

The inspector continues to question the "young prisoner."

"And so, my friend, you're innocent? Your face, I must say, hardly looks like that of a hardened criminal. For what crime were you convicted?"

"My word," Alice replies with imperturbable aplomb, "I don't really remember... A number of things..."

"You don't remember what you were convicted of?"

"Of course I don't remember, because I wasn't guilty."

"But that wouldn't prevent you..."

"Why should I remember the crimes of others?"

"This is all very confusing... Montpaillard Prison is decidedly a strange prison, and its director a bizarre functionary indeed!"

But Alice could not hear her friend criticized without protest.

"Don't say anything against Bluette," she cries. "He's such a great guy!"

Alas! Alice's courageous protestation has the opposite effect of her pure intentions!

The words "great guy," and especially the tone in which they were uttered, have unseeled[1] the inspector's eyes.

"Great guy?" he repeats. "The way you said that! But, may God pardon me... Would you be so kind as to remove your cap?"

"There, inspector, sir."

The brown cascade of Alice's hair unfurls onto her shoulders and back.

With infinite grace, the inspector doffs his hat as well.

He bows, and greets her:

"Madame!"

"Inspector, sir!" In the course of his career, the inspector had seen many odd things, but this, truly, surpassed the permissible limits of administrative fantasy.

A young woman, in a prisoner's uniform, reading *Figaro* and humming tunes from operettas, in a dark cell!

Not too banal, that!

The inspector is throughly baffled.

Hat in hand, he contemplates Alice, pretty little Alice, because she is pretty, the little minx, in her improvised disguise.

Ah, yes! The inspector is baffled.

But suddenly, his grave expression gives way to the brightest of smiles.

The old French gallantry has reclaimed its rights!

"You are delectable in that outfit, madame, but would you please tell me what curious chain of events led you into this uniform, and into this cell?"

"A simple personal whim, sir. I can assure you that M. Bluette was completely unaware of my little masquerade, and was as surprised as you to see me in these clothes..."

"Which suit you very well, besides. I would never have thought that clothes usually worn with such inelegance would be so attractive on a beautiful woman!"

"You flatter me, sir."

"No, I assure you. You look very nice."

"Well, since you think I'm so nice, promise me that you won't be too harsh with M. Bluette, who is such a great guy!"

"I promise... You seem to like him very much, your dear Bluette?"

"Very, very much!"

"Lucky man! You are charming, madame."

To prove his genuine sympathy, he takes Alice's hand, and holds it in his.

"You are positively charming."

"So, you won't scold him?"

"Don't worry."

"And you might even give him a little promotion?"

"Oh, that would be more difficult."

"Couldn't you find him a nice prison in Paris?"

"On the Champs-Elysées?"

"Or in Passy, perhaps."

"My word, she's adorable!... I have an overwhelming urge to kiss you."

"I don't mind, but only if you don't forget the prison in Passy."

"I swear!"

And, completely disarmed, the inspector kissed the young woman.

---

1. "Unseeled" is a term of falconry which is incorrectly spelled "unsealed." The word "seel" means to sew the eyelids of a bird of prey in order to train it... Read and learn!

Chapter XXIII

In which it is demonstrated administratively that it is sometimes as difficult to enter a prison as to leave one.

Invoking once again that curious privilege that I mentioned earlier, which confers on novelists the power to play with time as well as space, I will, ladies and gentlemen, with your permission, make you twenty-four hours younger for just a moment.

Let us take up things as they were when our old comrade Jules Fléchard, after the impressive scene of declarations at the Chaville residence, headed resolutely for the public prosecutor, sustained by both the sweet recollection of Arabella murmuring "Courage, my friend" (and heavens, in what a voice!) and by the civic exhortations of M. Guilloche, his impromptu attorney.

At the public prosecutor's office, these two gentlemen received a chilly reception.

In the absence of the public prosecutor, an old court clerk tried to convince them of the inanity of their actions.

"Take my advice, my friends, and just go home and forget it."

"But..."

"That would be more reasonable. The court made a mistake, you say, in convicting Blaireau instead of you. It's entirely possible; but that's between this Blaireau and you, M. Fléchard."

"The issue is more important," protested the lawyer.

"No, my dear counselor, the issue is not as important as you say it is. Blaireau served three months in prison for the sake of M. Fléchard, so it's up to the latter to make reparations to Blaireau. At twenty sous a day (and that's well paid), that gives us ninety francs. Let's say a hundred francs to make it a round number. Give Blaireau a hundred francs and forget about the whole business!"

"We'll come back tomorrow morning, and we'll see if the public prosecutor makes the same argument as you."

"If he doesn't, he'll be mistaken, and will serve the interests of justice very badly, interests that are more considerable and more august than those of a simple citizen such as you, M. Fléchard, no offense intended."

And, rising, the old clerk indicated that the conversation was over.

The gymnastics instructor spent a restless night.

If the judges refused to take his confession seriously, and didn't agree to put him in prison, what would Arabella de Chaville say?

For what she loved in him — as he knew full well — was the victim, as much as the hero.

No prison, no marriage.

The romantic young lady could do without high birth or nobility, but not the halo!

A halo! A martyr's halo, that's what Fléchard needed, at all costs!

A halo! A halo! My kingdom for a halo!

And so, the next morning, he knocked at the door of the public prosecutor's office.

"Ah!" cried the magistrate. "You're the aforesaid Fléchard (Jules)! Well, the aforesaid Fléchard (Jules) has missed a good opportunity to keep quiet! Just at vacation time! This is the season that you choose to get up to mischief!"

Fléchard replied with his head bowed:

"Sir, remorse cannot choose its day."

"Remorse? Oh, don't talk to me about remorse. Remorse for what? For having slugged that idiot constable? For having allowed that scoundrel Blaireau to be convicted in your place? None of it is of the slightest importance. Go, my friend, go back home, and let's have no more of your ridiculous story!"

"I do apologize, sir, for not sharing your opinion, but I insist on being imprisoned as soon as possible."

"Imprisoned? No! Committed to an insane asylum, maybe! Go away, my friend, go away!"

"Sir, I warn you that if you don't put me in prison, I'll appeal to higher jurisdiction."

"They'll send you packing."

"I shall not be refused:

    And I shall not stop, in short,

    Till I reach the highest court."

"Listen, Fléchard, can't you be reasonable, and put this business off until later, after vacation?"

"I intend to sleep in prison this very night."

"I'm beginning to think that I have a dangerous monomaniac before me. What you need is a cold shower!"

"Thank you, but I took one this morning."

"Not cold enough, apparently. Go away!"

And, seizing Fléchard by the arm, the magistrate shoved our poor friend out the door.

....

That afternoon, Fléchard made a heroic decision.

After having packed a little bag of clothes and toiletries, he headed for the prison.

M. Bluette, he thought to himself, is an excellent fellow. I know him, and he won't refuse to admit me into his establishment, at least for a few days.

On his way, he met the mayor, who, fuming with rage, said:

"Ah, there you are! I hope you're proud of yourself! There are three hundred imbeciles in front of the prison, waiting for Blaireau to be released, so they can carry him in triumph."

Despite his troubles, Fléchard could not help

laughing.

"That will be pretty funny!" he said.

"Pretty funny, indeed. Ah! If we only had the army in Montpaillard, I'd have all those idiots shot!"

"You don't fool around, Your Honor!"

"Come now, Fléchard, let's be serious. Do you still insist on claiming you're guilty? There's still time."

"More than ever, Your Honor, and I'm on my way to make myself a prisoner."

"Well then, I hope that all of the disorder that revolutionizes Montpaillard comes crashing onto your head!"

At the prison, Fléchard found Bluette, tormented, worried, and, rare for him, in a thoroughly foul mood.

And he had his reasons! That inspector, who just happened to find Alice dressed as a prisoner! What would be the result of that encounter? My God! My God! He would probably be fired.

"You, Fléchard! What do you want?"

"I suppose that you've kept abreast of the situation, sir?"

"The Blaireau affair, yes; you're the guilty party?"

"Perfectly."

"So?"

"So?... I wish to be admitted as a prisoner."

"Do you have a paper?"

"No, sir."

"A letter, something from the public prosecutor?"

"I have nothing."

"And you imagine that I'll lock you up, just like

that? My word, you amaze me!"

"So, now one needs a recommendation to get into prison?"

"Of course!"

"Always favoritism, then! Nepotism! Poor, poor France!"

"Goodbye, Fléchard. Learn to live with it."

"So it's understood then, you won't admit me?"

"No, as I already told you!... Stop bothering me!"

There was a knock at the office door.

"Ah, it's you again, Blaireau. What do you want?"

"I don't mean this as a reproach, sir, but it seems that you're taking your time to release me!"

"Impossible until I receive the order from the public prosecutor."

"Oh, damn it all! This is too much! Not only have I finished my sentence, but I'm recognized as innocent, and you still won't let me go! It's too much! Damn it all to hell and back! It's too much! I've never seen anything like this!"

"My case," cried Fléchard, "is even worse! I'm guilty and they won't lock me up!"

"My poor friend," said Bluette, "if we had to put all the guilty people in prison, we could never do it!"

"Ah, there's justice for you! Poor France!"

And he murmured:

"What will Arabella think?"

Blaireau, in his turn, had reached the acme of exasperation.

"Ah yes, poor France! You can say that again! Just

wait until I get out of here, and then I'll rearrange your government for you!"

As for Fléchard, he returned home, even sadder and wearier than usual.

CHAPTER XXIV

*In which the reader will not only not witness the release of Blaireau,
but will see the unfortunate man locked in the darkest dungeon.*

The Blaireau affair began to create a stir in Mont-paillard. Never had the seventeen members of the revolutionary party had so much fun, and they whipped up, with diabolical skill, this agitation, which the mayor, M. Dubenoît, fought with all the energy of a desperate man.

The *Nord-et-Cher Clarion* had printed, around noon, a second edition even more incendiary than the first.

And illustrated!

Thanks to an old engraving, found in the printer's basement, Blaireau was depicted laden with chains, crouching in a hideous dungeon, lit by a window which was narrow, but outrageously barred.

Vermin of every description swarmed on the

humid floor of this *in pace*.

As a caption, these simple words: "An innocent man, in Montpaillard, at the end of the nineteenth century..."

A copy of the paper was brought to Blaireau by his friend Victor, the guard.

"Say, look at that, old man. What a head they've given you!"

"I don't agree," Blaireau answered firmly. "Me, I think it's a good likeness."

"My poor Blaireau!"

"Just you wait, Victor, I'll show them they should care about poor old Blaireau."

"What? You're about to leave and you're still not content!"

"No, damn it all, I'm not content! And I'll show them all what he's made of, poor old Blaireau!"

"Who are you so upset with?"

"Who am I upset with? With the people at the public prosecutor's office, with that old fool Dubenoît, with all those swine in the gendarmerie. You just wait until I get out!"

"You won't eat them alive?"

"No, I won't bother... You probably have me confused with someone else, my poor Victor. You probably think that I'm still the simple and banal Blaireau that I was before!"

"What? Do you plan to ascend the throne of France, now?"

"No, but I'm the standard bearer of the persecuted!"

"Heavens!"

"I'm an honorary president!"

"Goodness!"

"I'm the hero, do you hear me, the hero of a gala organized by a baron!"

"Damn!"

"And this is the Blaireau that they have the nerve not to release! Ah! They'll hear from me!"

Blaireau, intoxicated by his own words, had reached the last degree of exasperation, and his vociferous protests shook the walls of the prison.

....

In the course of his walks through the halls, fate brought him face to face with the inspector, who was continuing his tour with Bluette.

"What's all this noise? And this costume? Tell me, M. Bluette, who is this individual?"

Bluette hastened to reply to his inspector:

"This individual, sir... Well, in fact, this is the innocent man, the one that we were just talking about."

But the inspector wouldn't fall for that again.

He'd already tried that line, with Alice. It wouldn't work anymore!

"My dear M. Bluette, you're a charming man, but you lack invention. Whenever you don't know what to say about someone, you say: 'That's the innocent man...' Come up with a different joke now and then, my dear Bluette, please!"

"But I assure you, my dear inspector. Besides, you can ask him yourself."

"This individual, innocent? With that face and those rags, I'd never believe it! And besides, innocent or not, he's making an intolerable racket." And he turned angrily to Blaireau. "Say, you, isn't it about time you stopped yelling like that?"

"I'll yell like that all I want, and it won't be you, with your rosette, that can shut me up, you know-it-all! If anyone has a right to yell around here, it's me!"

"Oh, so that's the tone you want to take, my lad! Guard, handcuff this man and throw him in a cell, now!"

"The first one who touches me..."

Two guards, on the inspector's orders, had soon locked Blaireau in a cell, where he continued to exhale his most ringing invectives.

At that moment, two Englishmen appeared, carrying a letter from their consul, warmly recommending them to the director of the prison.

"What do you want with me?"

"It seems that you have an innocent chappie heah in Montpaillard Prison?"

"Yes, what of it?"

"We should like to see the innocent chappie."

The inspector had had enough.

"This is the last straw! The English are getting into it, now! You don't have any 'innocent chappies' in England, so you have to come to France?"

"Nao, theah are no innocent chappies in England!"

"Well, gentlemen, you can't see ours, because we locked him in a cell. Listen, that's him yelling! Can you hear him?"

"Aoh! Bizarre!"

And the Englishmen departed, baffled to the marrow at the way, admittedly strange, in which prison regulations are understood in some departments in France.

CHAPTER XXV

*In which the reader will agree, for once, with M. Dubenoît, and be
persuaded that Montpaillard is indeed undergoing a crisis.*

In accordance with the principle that a good joke
is not improved by prolongation, the incarceration of
the unfortunate Blaireau came to an end around five
o'clock that evening... The entire population of Montpaillard, usually so peaceful, has gathered around the
prison.

The revolutionary party, under the direction of
the ambitious Guilloche, is very vocal, hoping to give
to their modest numbers the appearance of a large
and disciplined crowd.

They almost achieve this result by recruiting, with
some misgivings, a handful of street urchins who are
delighted with the opportunity.

The mayor dreams of cavalry charges, machine
guns, arrests for sedition. Ah, if they only had the

army in Montpaillard!

Or if, at least, they still had Sergeant Martin, a man who knew his stuff, a fine man who studied police work in the famous brigades of the Paris suburbs, so renowned for their radical techniques of frightening the criminal and reassuring the virtuous!

Alas! The formidable Martin had retired over a year ago!

And there was nothing to set this rabble right, nothing but a bourgeois police force and a few lethargic mounted officers. Besides, they seemed to be having as much fun as the gawkers.

To make things worse, here comes Parju, the constable: Parju whose testimony led to Blaireau's conviction, and, thanks to that, this whole scandal.

The crowd boos Parju: "Hey, Parju, put on your glasses! Did you find your badge, Parju?" etc.

Parju eventually realizes that his presence is not ideal for calming the public, and selects a route toward the periphery (as a municipal councilman would say) of Montpaillard.

Suddenly the prison doors open, and a cry rings out: "Hooray for Blaireau! Hooray for Guilloche!" but especially: "Hooray for Blaireau!"

The two colleagues step forward, arm in arm: Guilloche serious in his sober black coat, Blaireau radiant and draped in the unnameable rags previously described.

It is a beautiful sight.

....

The two Englishmen are in the crowd: one takes notes, and the other operates his "bull's eye"[1] with unusual enthusiasm.

They seem particularly interested in Blaireau's rags.

They will not be believed when, having returned to the bosom of perfidious Albion, they will describe for their compatriots these scenes of judicial life in France.

....

But, bit by bit, order is restored to Montpaillard.

The peaceful citizens, gathered now around the familial soup, comment diversely on the day's events.

The fierce revolutionaries, assembled in the grand hall upstairs at the Future Bar, offer Blaireau a long series of celebratory vermouths, celebratory bitters, celebratory absinthes, and even celebratory quinines!

These assorted drinks soon provoke the assembled into saying terrible things about the government.

Completely at ease, a model of modesty, charming with everyone, Blaireau promises his protection to all.

Once back home, M. Dubenoît takes off his coat, mops his streaming brow, and falls, overwhelmed, into an armchair.

"My poor dear," he says to his wife, "there's no use pretending otherwise. Montpaillard is undergoing a crisis!"

---

1. A small camera which I cannot recommend too highly to my readers.

$\mathcal{C}$HAPTER $\mathcal{XXVI}$

In which a fine political future dawns on the horizon of Blaireau's destiny.

M. Dubenoît is right: it would be foolish to pretend otherwise, Montpaillard is undergoing a crisis.

Emotions are running high, the revolutionary party makes enormous progress.

At M. Guilloche's talk ("The miscarriage of justice through the ages, from Saint Louis's oak until today"), Blaireau debuted in his function as honorary president, with that delicious informality to which he has the secret, and which has won him so much acclaim.

A huge crowd for the speech; free shows are so rare in the provinces!

And besides, tomorrow is the great charity gala, on the Chaville grounds, for the honor and benefit of the unfortunate victim, and what an attractive program!

Opening of the grounds at two o'clock in the

afternoon, carnival booths, carousel, somnambulist, circus of the Molier type with local youths as artists; little girls selling flowers; rustic inn and American bar, both staffed by young ladies from the best families of Montpaillard, and a host of other amusements that it would be impossible to detail in advance.

In the evening, there will be a grand ball, and, to finish the gala, an exhibition of fireworks!

Concerning these fireworks, the Baron imagined a display that would be the high point, the sensational climax of these splendid festivities.

A heroic woman, depicted first in red lights, will then be lit in white, and will finish by bursting into pieces.

This pyrotechnic display — you understood the symbolism, I hope — is the innocence of Blaireau, which *bursts forth* to the eyes of all!

With no false modesty, the Baron shows himself quite proud of his creation, which everyone, around him, qualifies as simply inspired.

In short, no one will be bored tomorrow, and the attendees will get their hundred sous' worth, for the price of admission is set at five francs, which gives admittance to all of the booths, the carousel, and the ball.

Not to the refreshments, of course.

The Baron de Hautpertuis is an exemplary organizer: without really doing anything himself, he has the gift of galvanizing his collaborators, and inspiring limitless activity among the most indolent.

No detail escapes him, he thinks of everything, he anticipates everything.

"Ah! We almost forgot the police protection. And here's His Honor the Mayor, you come just at the right time."

"What can I do for you, Baron?"

"We need to talk about the police protection."

"That's exactly why I was looking for you. I hope to hide a few gendarmes in the flowerbeds. Do you have any objections?"

"On the contrary, gendarmes always look their best in flowerbeds."

"And I must also warn you that at the slightest trouble from your damned Blaireau, I'll have him arrested and imprisoned."

"Blaireau will behave. I'll see to that myself, my dear M. Dubenoît."

"I hope so, although I doubt it, since everyone is turning his head with all of these articles, these honorary presidencies, these revolutionary talks, these charity galas!... Ah, I can never repeat it enough! Montpaillard is undergoing a crisis!"

"As far as our gala is concerned, my dear M. Dubenoît, I must energetically protest."

"Don't protest, Baron. This gala is an immoral and antisocial demonstration, a gala for the profit of a criminal!"

"A criminal?... I beg your pardon."

"Not even!... A false criminal. God only knows where we're going! The values of my people have been perverted!"

"Do you want my opinion, M. Dubenoît? In your place, I'd be less disagreeable! Montpaillard is a calm little town, it's just bored. One need only walk around for a quarter of an hour to notice it. It's bored, and has probably been bored for a long time."

"Since Henri IV, in whose reign it was founded."

"That's an eternity! It's no surprise that it finally wants a little amusement. It took the first opportunity that came along. Just ask M. Guilloche. Good day, M. Guilloche! Our mayor was just lamenting the evil ideas that are beginning to manifest in the spirit of Montpaillard."

"Oh, yes," the young lawyer replied. "I believe, without flattering myself too much, that my talk on miscarriages of justice made a certain impression around here."

"I don't doubt it."

"And that in the next election, our party will get a few more than seventeen votes. What do you think, Your Honor?"

"I'm sure of it, my dear Guilloche, and I can't congratulate you enough on your magnificent unselfishness!"

"What do you mean?"

"I mean that you're well on your way to ensuring Blaireau's political future, for the people cry 'Hurray for Blaireau!' They carry Blaireau in triumph."

"That's true."

"And what about you, do they carry you in

triumph?"

"I've never sought that kind of popularity."

"It's a good thing, Guilloche, a very good thing, to sacrifice oneself for one's convictions, and Blaireau will be deeply indebted to you when he's elected to Parliament."

"Blaireau in Parliament! You're joking, Your Honor!"

"Not in the least, and, deep down, I'm delighted with the turn that things have taken."

"Ah... Delighted?"

"Perfectly so. The arrondissement of Montpaillard will be represented by an innocent man. This will not pass unnoticed in the House, and will, I hope, bring some glory to our unfortunate country."

"Blaireau in Parliament! You're mad!"

And Guilloche went on his way, affected, all the same, by a reverie that bordered on apprehension.

*C*HAPTER XXVII

In which, by special favor, the reader will be introduced, before the gates open, into the heart of the gala given for the honor and benefit of Blaireau.

"Ladies and gentlemen, the gala is shaping up splendidly!"

"Oh yes, Baron, and superb weather, besides!"

"Well, not's not waste time. It's half past one, and the gate opens at exactly two o'clock. Let's not let the crowd get ahead of us. Ladies and gentlemen, please take your positions at your respective counters. Officers, where are the officers?"

Several big louts stepped forward.

"Here we are, Baron."

"Ah, perfect! Do you have your badges, gentlemen?"

"Yes, Baron."

"So all is going well... I don't see our little barmaids."

"They're still putting on their aprons."

Several young women arrived, as pretty as a picture, and so fresh!

"Ah, here they are! They're charming, our little barmaids! You understand, ladies, don't you? All of the drinks cost one franc. Sell champagne, ladies, and sell a lot of it. Drive the men to intemperance!... In fact, how is the champagne?"

"Try some, Baron."

M. de Hautpertuis takes a sip and tries to suppress a grimace:

"Oh! Not so great, this champagne. But for a gala like this, it's all we need."

"One franc, Baron, if you please!"

"Here's your franc, mademoiselle. Drive the men to intemperance. You won't have much trouble, anyway, in this heat!... But where's our Blaireau? I don't see Blaireau!"

"Blaireau?" replied M. de Chaville. "He's hard at work, busily engaged in drinking a cup of excellent coffee, in which he emptied half a carafe of my oldest brandy."

"Bring him here!... Officer, please find Blaireau for me."

Here's Blaireau!

Blaireau decked out in an antique, but still superb, frock coat, which comes from his lawyer's closet.

A large red dahlia adorns his buttonhole. A top hat, slightly out of date, is pulled down over his liberally pomaded hair.

With a persistence worthy of a better object, our

poor friend is trying to force his huge mitts into gloves the color of fresh butter (not too fresh).

Blaireau's arrival elicits a murmur of appreciation, to which he responds with a few condescending nods.

The Baron alone does not approve. He severely adjusts his monocle, examines Blaireau, and renders his judgment:

"My dear Blaireau, you should present yourself to the populace in tails."

"In tails?"

"Yes, in tails! Oh, I know you'll tell me, my dear friend, that tails are not worn in the afternoon. Your objection would be perfectly reasonable at any other time, but, given the circumstances that gather us here today, the case is completely different. The beneficiary of a charity gala must wear white tie and tails."

"I have no objection, Baron, but I don't have anything like that in my modest wardrobe."

"M. Chaville would take great pleasure in loaning you one. You're about the same size. Isn't that right, Chaville?"

"I'll be happy to!... Placide, give my tailcoat to M. Blaireau. (*In a low voice to Placide.*) Number three."

Even in a number three tailcoat, Blaireau looks magnificent.

He hooks his thumbs in the armholes of his waistcoat, and takes a few steps to show off his appearance.

New acclamations.

A single critical voice is raised, that of M. Dubenoît. The bitter mayor can barely conceal his mounting rage.

"Ah yes, a fine outfit to represent the persecuted!"

"Excuse me, Your Honor," Blaireau judiciously observed, "let's not confuse things, please. Here I'm not the standard bearer for the persecuted, but the hero of a gala given in my honor and for my benefit... In my honor, Mayor, and for my benefit! That bothers you, eh, papa Dubenoît?"

M. Dubenoît shrugs his mute and angry shoulders.

The mayor had brought his constable with him.

"An excellent idea!" the Baron says. "We'll put him at the gate... That way, the other officers will be free to circulate, and to enjoy the gala. Is he intelligent, your constable?"

"He's not intelligent, and I'm all the prouder of him for it. He's better than intelligent, he's disciplined."

"Congratulations! That's enough for the mission that we'll give him... Constable!"

"Yes, Baron?"

"Pay close attention to what I tell you."

"Yes, Baron."

"You will sit at this desk, next to this gate. You will collect five francs from every person who enters, except, of course, those that are lending their support to the gala, barmaids, musicians, young people from the circus, etc. Do you understand, my friend?"

"Perfectly, Baron, I understand."

"Repeat your orders."

"Collect a hundred sous from everybody, except those that are lending their support."

"Perfectly. Now go to your post, because it's already two o'clock. The crowd will soon flock to us."

....

However, the crowd did not flock.

No paying creature has yet appeared at the gate, and it's getting late.

M. Dubenoît would have laughed heartily into his beard, if he had a beard, but, unfortunately, he was clean-shaven.

Ah! Here are a few people!

It's M. Guilloche and his family.

After a brief exchange with the constable, all of these people enter without paying; Guilloche insists on explaining.

"We took the liberty, my dear Blaireau, my family and I, to enter your gala without paying..."

"But you did the right thing, M. Guilloche, you did the right thing!... How do I look?"

"Splendid, Blaireau, splendid! Obviously, you were born to wear tails."

"I hear you! These look better than those filthy rags that you put me in the other day, eh, you rascal?"

Since leaving prison, Blaireau had become extraordinarily friendly with his lawyer.

He showered him with pokes and slaps, called him names bordering on the vulgar, and even assumed a patronizing air that eventually irritated Guilloche.

And besides, let us repeat, Blaireau's growing popularity was a matter of some concern to our ambitious young attorney.

Blaireau in Parliament! Who can say, with universal suffrage?

$\mathcal{C}$HAPTER XXVIII

In which Blaireau demonstrates an uncommon nobility of soul, and a willingness to forget insults which is absolutely Christian.

"Well!" Blaireau suddenly cried. "A watering hole! That's a fine idea, putting a watering hole in the gala!"

It was the American bar that Blaireau designated with the rather popular sobriquet of "watering hole."

"And in fact, my thirst is killing me."

He went up to it, and ordered a glass of champagne, which vanished down his throat with extraordinary speed.

"They're remarkably small, these glasses, mademoiselle."

"Drink two then, M. Blaireau!"

"I could ask for nothing better."

"After all that you've suffered, M. Blaireau, you have the right to two glasses of champagne."

"Ah yes, I suffered! Good God almighty how I

suffered, my little mademoiselle."

"Poor M. Blaireau!"

"That was what one might call a harsh captivity!"

And Blaireau is perfectly sincere as he heaves a sigh in memory of his undeserved tortures: after hearing it repeated so many times, after seeing himself pitied by so many compassionate souls, he believes, with all his heart, that it happened!

"Poor M. Blaireau!" repeated the charming young barmaid.

"Ah yes, mademoiselle, you might well say 'Poor M. Blaireau!' You don't know how I suffered in prison! Will you drink a toast with me, mademoiselle?"

Elise (she answered to the sweet name of Elise) apologized that she could not accept the invitation.

"Thank you, M. Blaireau, but I never take anything between meals."

"You're mistaken, mademoiselle, for it may be a long time before you get another chance to have a drink with a martyr! In fact, here's my lawyer!"

"M. Guilloche?"

"Himself. I don't know what's wrong with him the past few days, he's not the same with me. Hey there, lawyer man!"

"Are you speaking to me?" Guilloche curtly replied.

"Of course to you! Who did you expect? How about a drink with me, while you're here?"

"Impossible. As you can see, I'm with these women."

"Well, the ladies aren't in the way. The more

the merrier!"

Guilloche walked away without a reply.

One of the women remarked:

"He's not very distinguished, your protégé."

"My protégé? More like my protector, for it seems that the Blaireau candidacy is making enormous progress, from what I hear on all sides."

"To the detriment of yours?"

"Of course."

"I'm delighted to hear it, my dear M. Guilloche. Perhaps this misadventure will bring you back to the conservative party."

"I won't contradict you."

"Our great conservative party, without which France would not be France."

"Obviously! Obviously!"

But what do you expect of a lawyer's convictions?

It is only right to add that the ethics of certain magistrates are just as variable, and perhaps a bit flabby, if I may say so.

Take as an example that excellent judge of the Montpaillard court, M. Lerechigneux, who, at that very moment, made his entrance into the gala.

Blaireau spotted him immediately.

Joy in his heart, grown more gregarious by the glasses of champagne that he had just swallowed in rapid succession, Blaireau, his hand open wide, rushed over to M. Lerechigneux.

"Hello, Your Honor, how are you?"

"Monsieur..."

"I'll bet that you don't recognize me."

"Your face, sir, is not completely unfamiliar to me, but I must admit that I don't recall exactly under what circumstances and where I had the honor..."

"The honor! Ha ha! That's a good one!... The honor!"

Poor M. Lerechigneux, despite desperate efforts, is unable to recognize this gentleman in white tie and tails. "Some gentleman farmer," he thinks.

"I don't mean this as a reproach," smiles Blaireau, "but you're certainly friendlier today, Your Honor, than the day when you had... the honor, as you put it, to procure for me three months of you know what."

Then, with a bow, he gravely introduces himself:

"M. Blaireau!"

"Ah, of course! It's funny, I didn't recognize you. How are you, M. Blaireau?"

"Very well, thank you... It's not surprising that you didn't remember me, Your Honor, since the day when you had the honor... I was not as well dressed."

"Indeed, I don't remember exactly what clothes you were wearing, but I don't think that you were in tails."

"Or a white tie, either, but that's the way it is! One day, you're in your shirtsleeves, treated like the lowest of the low. Three months later, you're in white tie and tails, and everyone calls you Monsieur Blaireau, all hoity toity."

"That's life!... And who do you have to thank for it, dear M. Blaireau? Me."

"You, Your Honor?"

"Why, certainly, me. Because, after all, if you hadn't been found guilty in the first place, you couldn't have been found innocent after that, and nobody would have paid any attention to you."

"That's true, in fact."

"That's why, my dear Blaireau, I thought I had the right to enter without paying."

"You did the right thing, Your Honor."

"Well, I see that you don't hold a grudge against me for our little misunderstanding."

"Me, hold a grudge against you! And for what?... You found me guilty, because you're a judge... If you'd been a lawyer, you'd have found me innocent... Everyone has his specialty!"

"It's a pleasure, my dear M. Blaireau, to hear a man discuss things with such common sense."

"And the proof, Your Honor, that I don't hold a grudge against you, is that we'll have a drink together."

"With pleasure."

"Mademoiselle, two glasses of champagne."

"Here you are, M. Blaireau."

Blaireau raises his glass, and proclaims:

"To justice!"

M. Lerechigneux does the same, and replies:

"To innocence!"

They clink their glasses.

"And now, my dear M. Blaireau, I shall leave you, to enjoy this gala given in your honor."

"In my honor, and for my benefit, Your Honor.

Have a good time, and above all try to stir up business."

CHAPTER XXIX

In which things begin to go sour between Blaireau and his ex-accuser, the constable Parju (Ovide).

M. Dubenoît had warned his constable.

"Your mission is a delicate one, my dear Parju."

"Yes, Your Honor!"

"It's possible, it's even probable, that in the course of this gala, Blaireau may indulge in a bit of raillery at your expense."

"A bit of... what, if you please, Your Honor?"

"A bit of raillery, that is, jokes in poor taste, ridicule, insults."

"Very well, Your Honor."

"You will answer nothing, nothing, nothing! Is that understood?"

"Understood, Your Honor."

"Not a word."

"Yes, Your Honor."

"Not even a gesture."

"Yes, Your Honor."

"However, if this citizen makes a single misstep, you will inform me immediately."

"Yes, Your Honor."

Parju summarized his orders to himself in a phrase that Tacitus would have envied: "Neither word, nor gesture," and awaited further developments.

Further developments did not leave him waiting long.

Very proud at having clinked glasses with the judge, Blaireau could not resist the temptation to gloat over it to Parju, who had seen the scene from afar.

Without leaving the bar, he called to the humble functionary.

"Hey, old pal, what do you say to that?"

Parju did not respond.

"You see who I drank with. With the chief justice of the Montpaillard court. Are you the one clinking glasses with the chief justice of the court? Eh, wise guy?"

Parju did not respond.

"You, you probably couldn't even have a drink with the court clerk."

Parju did not respond.

Blaireau hesitated a moment between two options: to lose his temper at the stubborn man, or to take pity on the stupid one.

The generous option prevailed.

"Come on, old brother of mine, I don't hold a

grudge... Have a drink with me, just the two of us."

Parju did not respond.

"Mademoiselle, two glasses of champagne, please... Here's to you, Parju!"

Parju did not respond.

"You don't want to toast?... Well, here's to you, anyway."

And Blaireau emptied the two glasses, muttering:

"What an idiot."

Then he added:

"You have to wonder if the government isn't crazy, hiring constables of that caliber!"

Chapter XXX

In which, or rather, at the end of which, the stainless memory of Agrippa d'Aubigné will be lightly tarnished, but not very much, really.

"Say, but I recognize you!" said Blaireau to the slender gentleman who was approaching with such a sorrowful expression.

Jules Fléchard, for it was he, rummaged through the drawers of his memory, but in vain: he, for his part, did not recognize his interlocutor.

"Wasn't it you," continued the latter, "who wanted to enter prison, at all costs, just as I was trying to leave?"

"M. Blaireau, I presume."

"Himself, in person."

"I'm delighted to make your acquaintance."

"Me too, I'm delighted, but, if you don't mind my saying so, you could have made my acquaintance a little earlier. It wouldn't have been too hard. You knew where to find me."

He assumed a supremely ironic expression.

"I barely moved, you know, for three months."

"I preferred to wait."

"To wait for what?"

"The right time."

"That's a funny idea!... Well, each to his own. A glass of champagne with me, just the two of us, my dear... What's your name again?"

"Fléchard... Jules Fléchard."

"My dear Fléchard, to show you that I don't hold a grudge; I don't know what's wrong with me today, I can't hold a grudge against anyone, even that old fool of a constable. Eh, Parju?"

Parju did not respond.

Fléchard was going to politely accept Blaireau's gracious invitation, when he paled as he perceived Arabella de Chaville come toward him.

"Mademoiselle!"

"M. Fléchard! (*Whispered*) Jules."

"(*Whispered*) Arabella!... Imagine my distress! Yesterday, I made another valiant attempt at the public prosecutor's office; those swine refuse to incarcerate me... Rest assured, dear one, that, this past week, I've made infinitely more efforts to enter prison than it would have taken me to avoid it."

The face of the aging but romantic young woman was suffused with a charming blush.

"Listen, Jules, I've given the matter some serious thought these past few days, I've questioned myself seriously, and (*lowering her voice and blushing even more*) I would now prefer that we not be separated, my friend."

Fléchard trembled with joy:

"Arabella, you're an angel!" And he kissed her hand.

"And you, Jules, are my hero!"

"Yes, Arabella, we shall be happy... But when?"

"Soon, Jules."

"Not before I've paid my debt."

"What debt?"

"My debt to society. Until now, I never owed anything to society, but now I must settle up."

"It doesn't matter. I have a sort of premonition that this business will work itself out."

M. Lerechigneux was passing by.

"Isn't that right, Your Honor, that this business will work itself out?"

"In principle, mademoiselle, all business works itself out, but what sort of business are you referring to at the moment?"

"The case of M. Fléchard, the guilty party in the Blaireau affair."

Blaireau had heard.

"The Blaireau affair!" he repeated like an echo, more and more heated by champagne. "Ah, that's an affair worthy of the name, that one, the Blaireau affair! But the Fléchard affair, that, that's nothing at all. Your Honor will agree with me: the Fléchard affair, that, that's nothing at all. Ah, I'd rather hear about the Blaireau affair."

"Blaireau is correct," confirmed the judge. "M. Fléchard has a right to expect leniency from the court. Three months of prison have already been served for the crime. (*To Fléchard.*) The court will keep you in mind, and I think that I can tell you that with a small fine..."

"A fine!"

"Around sixteen francs..."

"Oh, thank you, Your Honor!" cried Arabella. "Your words are a balm to my heart!"

Blaireau, who felt decidedly sympathetic to Fléchard, proposed:

"There's something even simpler, and that would be to acquit him. What if we just acquitted him right now, Your Honor, while we empty a glass? Let's agree, eh, we acquit Fléchard!"

"Here, my dear friend, it wouldn't count; but I repeat, the court will be lenient, I can promise."

"Even more so," mitigated Fléchard with a detached expression, "because the thing is insignificant. In the Middle Ages nobody would have even noticed it. It was the favorite pastime of the great lords to beat their constables; Colbert, Sully, Agrippa d'Aubigné had no other amusement!"

"Oh," protested the judge, "not Agrippa d'Aubigné!... I don't know if Agrippa d'Aubigné..."

"Yes sir, he would," affirmed Blaireau. "Agrippa d'Aubigné like everybody else!... Mademoiselle, serve us four glasses of champagne! It's been too long since we had a toast!"

And he added happily:

"Agrippa d'Aubigné, I knew him way back when. He was one tough customer!"

Chapter XXXI

In which the director of Montpaillard Prison shows himself still faithful to his system of employing prisoners in the profession that they practiced before their arrest.

Meanwhile, Blaireau continued to be the best customer at the bar.

He told the young lady acting as barmaid:

"Keep track of my drinks, mademoiselle, I'll pay my little bill this evening, when I get my proceeds."

Up until then, the proceeds didn't seem to be reaching vertiginous heights, and in spite of the repeated "It's going well, it's going well," from our optimistic Baron, customers persisted in being very sparse indeed.

Blaireau showed a remarkable insistence on not "doing the Swiss," as they say in the barracks, that is, in not drinking alone.

Every new arrival, he invited.

"The least I can do is stand for the drinks today!

Mademoiselle and you, my dear old Fléchard, have another glass of champagne."

"I don't want to offend you, M. Blaireau," said Arabella, "but..."

"That's right, it wouldn't be nice to offend me, after all I've suffered."

"You exaggerate, M. Blaireau, you didn't suffer as much as you claim. And besides, quite often, you received little treats, wine, cigars, and jam."

"That's true... How the devil did you know that?"

Embarrassed, she stammered:

"I know that, because..."

Fléchard came to his friend's assistance:

"Mademoiselle is the president of a society devoted to helping all of the innocent men and women in our prisons."

"Well, well, well! I never heard of this organization."

"It's called the 'League to Rectify as Far as Possible the Disadvantages of Miscarriages of Justice.'"

"It must keep busy, your league! But, in fact, mademoiselle, how did you know that I was innocent?"

"Ah, well! Our league has its spies."

"But you, my poor Fléchard, I guess nobody will send you cigars during your harsh imprisonment?"

"Alas, no! Me, I'm a genuine criminal."

"Don't be too upset, I'll recommend you to my former boss. He'll take care of you. Hey, M. Bluette, may I have a word with you, please?... Don't you recognize your former guest?"

"My word, I swear, I didn't recognize you. Damn, old man, just look at the way you're dressed!"

"It was nice, I must say, for you to come to my gala."

"I insisted on coming to shake your hand. Having known you when you were in trouble, I'm delighted to contemplate you in triumph. I'll even admit, my dear Blaireau, that I took the liberty of entering without paying."

"And you did the right thing, M. Bluette!... Why, that would have been something... Did you ever ask me for a sou, the whole time that I was in your establishment?"

"Not once, as a matter of fact! What's more, two of my guests have made a request which I found myself unable to refuse. They're waiting for me at the gate."

The Baron de Hautpertuis could not suppress a vague feeling of concern.

"You brought two of your prisoners here, to this gala?"

"Two charming boys, Baron, whom Blaireau knew at my place, Feston and Durenfort."

"Yes," affirmed Blaireau, "two nice guys, and not stuck up at all."

"Would you be so kind, Baron, as to loan them a booth to permit them to practice their curious exercises?"

"What do these exercises consist of?"

"One of them plays slide trombone, while the other eats live rabbits."

"Live rabbits? Poor creatures!" moaned one of the

young barmaids.

"Oh. they're used to it, mademoiselle, they're used to it!"

"Your performers, maybe, but not the rabbits."

"And," inquired the Baron, "of what crime were these artists convicted?"

"The trombonist for having nocturnally borrowed a neighbor's rabbit, and the other for having eaten it."

"Of course!" said M. Lerechigneux. "I remember, I was the one who convicted them. I identified, quite ingeniously, the second as a receiver of stolen goods."

"Quite ingenious, indeed. Over here, my friends, over here."

"A glass of champagne before you go," Blaireau did not forget.

"I won't say no to that."

"Good old Feston! Good old Durenfort!"

"Good old Blaireau!"

CHAPTER XXXII

In which Blaireau builds a beautiful dream which collapses no sooner than hatched, if the reader will excuse the expression.

The author has delayed as long as possible the promulgation of a fact which is rather painful, but unfortunately impossible to conceal any longer.

Blaireau is now completely drunk, as drunk as the entire country of Poland, back when there was a Poland, and when Poland was happy.

From the cordiality that it expressed at first, Blaireau's intoxication quickly turned to annoying familiarity: it was starting to verge on rudeness.

Our friend walks around the gala, around his gala, a deck of cards in his hand, and stops people: "Take one." Someone takes a card. "It's the eight of clubs!" he cries triumphantly, or "The king of hearts," depending on the occasion.

And the most curious thing is that Blaireau is

always right.

Another of Blaireau's unknown talents!

And then Blaireau beams: he's going to be rich, very rich!

The Chaville grounds, suddenly, are full of people. All of Montpaillard is there, in the booths or on the carousel.

At five francs apiece, what a take!

What will he do with all that money?

Hey, by God! He'll buy a bar. An excellent idea.

As popular as he is, he's sure to attract a large clientele as soon as it opens.

Ah, for an idea, that's an idea, and a superb one!

"Say, papa Dubenoît, you know what? Well! With all my money, I'm going to open a cafe, a pretty little cafe, the Blaireau cafe!"

"It will be very nice, I'm sure, your Blaireau cafe!"

"A little cafe, just across from the courthouse, with a sign reading: 'At the rendezvous of the innocents!' What do you think of that, eh?"

"I think that your establishment won't stay open long, that's what I think."

"And who will close it, may I ask?"

"Myself, my dear friend, and I can assure you that it won't take long."

"If you ever do that, my good man, do you know what will happen?"

"It doesn't matter!"

"What will happen is that I'll be named mayor in your place."

On hearing these words, the Baron burst out laughing:

"Blaireau mayor!... Then Montpaillard would really be undergoing a crisis, my dear M. Dubenoît!"

"Ah, Baron!" groaned Dubenoît. "We live in troubled times!"

"I don't agree... Just look at how much fun all these people are having! Having fun, that's the important thing!"

"You're right, Baron, old boy!" cried Blaireau. "Let's live it up! Serious business tomorrow!... By the way, would it be indiscreet to ask how much my take is at the moment?"

"We'll do the accounting this evening, after we close."

"I'd still like to know where we stand now."

"Nothing could be easier, we'll simply ask the constable. He's the one I posted to collect the admission... Parju!"

"Yes, Baron?"

"Could you please tell me how much money we have in the till?"

"How much money?... But... Not a sou, Baron!"

"Not a sou!"

"Not a sou, Baron, not a sou!"

CHAPTER XXXIII

In which Blaireau's ruin is revealed as total.

Not a sou!

The worst of it was that this declaration was not a joke, as Blaireau and the Baron thought at first.

It was the truth, the terrible truth!

Parju had let everyone in without paying.

Besides, the explanation that he offered for his behavior was of the simplest:

"The Baron told me not to charge admission to anyone who was lending support to the gala. So I asked everyone: 'Are you lending your support?' And they said: 'What support?' And I said: 'Because, you see, if you aren't lending your support, you have to pay five francs; if you are lending your support, you get in free.' And everyone answered: 'I'm lending my support.'"

"And so, nobody paid?"

"Nobody, Baron, nobody!"

"Ah!" cried Dubenoît, laughing, "now I understand why there was such a crowd!"

"Imbecile! You swine, Parju!"

Red enough to burst, fists clenched, Blaireau rolled his eyes in fury:

"Fool! Triple fool! Swine! It wasn't enough to convict me unjustly, now you have to ruin me, too! Now you have to throw me into the poorhouse! Ah, if I don't control myself!"

And with those words, Blaireau no longer controls himself, but throws himself upon Parju, whom he favors with numerous blows, to the chest as well as to the face.

A crowd gathers.

"Gendarmes!" cries Dubenoît in triumph, "arrest this man!... Ah, my boy, now you can't deny that you assaulted a constable, a sworn functionary!"

Those who had not witnessed the scene inquire:

"What's wrong? What happened?"

"Blaireau just attacked the constable."

"Again? This is getting to be an obsession!" Jules Fléchard cynically remarked.

The two Englishmen whom we met in earlier chapters (decidedly, one meets Englishmen everywhere!) had at that very moment arrived at the gala.

They asked someone:

"Pahdon me, old bean, but wheah is the innocent chappie?"

"There he is, gentlemen, between the two gendarmes."

"Oh deah! Awfully curious! Frawnce is a droll
country indeed!"

CHAPTER XXXIV

In which all is resolved, and not too badly, at that.

Blaireau realized that resistance was futile.

Suddenly sober, solidly grasped by the harsh fist of the gendarmes, his only thought was to get out of this unfortunate situation as advantageously as possible.

Noticing M. Guilloche in the crowd, he implored him:

"My lawyer! Please, get me released."

"I'm no longer your lawyer."

"Since when?"

"Since you became guilty."

"There's a lawyer for you!... He abandons his clients when they need him the most! You're a strange lawyer!"

"And you're a strange client!"

"My lawyer abandons me! My God, what's to

become of me? All that's left is to plead with the court. I beg of you, judge, Your Honor, have them release me."

"Your request is perfectly reasonable, my dear friend. Gendarmes, set M. Blaireau free."

"I formally object!" protested the mayor.

"You're wrong, Your Honor! This man having previously atoned for the crime that he just committed, it's in the interest of justice to acknowledge the situation. Blaireau owes no debt to society: he paid in advance."

"Well put, Your Honor!" cried Blaireau.

Impressed by the judge's noble, just, and generous words, the gendarmes relinquished Blaireau.

Exhausted, completely demoralized, the poor lad collapses into a chair.

"Ruined!" he sobs. "And my political career compromised?"

"I should say so!" Dubenoît replies in triumph.

"My God, what's to become of me? Ah, I'm so discouraged!... Baron, could you find a little position for me in Paris, by any chance?"

"In Paris?"

"Yes, in Paris, because I can't think of staying in Montpaillard... With all the jealousies I've stirred up around here!"

"A position... I'll think it over, my friend."

"As soon as possible, please, Baron."

"Of course, but I'm thinking... You do card tricks?"

"That's all that's left to me in my despair."

"You wear a suit admirably well!"

"Everyone complimented me on that."

"Well then! I'll get you work as a croupier in a little circle that I know in Cabourg."

"Can you put money aside in that kind of work?"

"Up your sleeves, even!"

"All right, it's fine with me."

Now, Blaireau feels somewhat reassured.

He replaces, in his buttonhole, the big faded red dahlia with another bigger, fresher, and redder dahlia.

And he cries cheerfully:

"I knew it, by God! Innocence is always rewarded!"

$\mathcal{C}$HAPTER ∞ $\mathcal{XXXV}$

In which the author, having concluded Blaireau's judiciary adventures, quickly liquidates the accounts of several other heroes who are less important, but still not entirely devoid of interest.

A few months after the events which have just taken place above, Jules Fléchard led to the altar his beloved, radiant in her white dress, sparkling with happiness and love.

Marriage, whatever the detractors of that fine institution may say, possesses several advantages, among them the fact that it can transform, from one day to the next, an old maid into a young wife, provided, of course, that the old maid does not yet enjoy too pronounced a state of senility.

Mlle. Arabella de Chaville, a little ridiculous in her white wedding dress, quickly changed into a Mme. Jules Fléchard in pearl gray silk, who was utterly charming.

Where do you think the newlyweds ran to enjoy

their honeymoon in private?

To Venice, you guessed it, to Venice, where they became drunk on love, on gondolas, on sensual Neapolitan songs, and on the *tutti frutti* at the Cafe Florian.

They did not have many children, but were happy anyway, which is less inconvenient.

Let us envy these two creatures, whose dreams came true, and return to Paris.

There we have the opportunity to see our old acquaintance, the amiable director of Montpaillard Prison, M. Bluette.

Thanks to a thoroughly glowing report from that gallant inspector, whose visit, I hope, you have not forgotten, M. Bluette received a promotion.

He is currently in the central administration, with an excellent salary and, even better, very little to do.

The Baron de Hautpertuis, who has become quite attached to him, often meets him at his office, and takes him to dinner in some fashionable cabaret, in the company of Delphine de Serquigny, who is more delectable than ever.

These three characters seem to get along famously.

TRANSLATOR'S NOTES

A FEW LINES FROM THE AUTHOR: Tristan Bernard was an old friend of Allais. The two collaborated on two short plays, *Silvérie* (1898) and *Congé amiable* (1903), both based on short stories by Allais. In fact, it's likely that Bernard did most of the work.

François-René de Chateaubriand, an early and influential Romantic, is buried on the tidal island of Grand Bé, near Saint-Malo.

CHAPTER I: Henry Bauër was a theater critic, well known for his progressive ideas on both art and politics. He was the only critic to give Alfred Jarry's *Ubu Roi* a favorable review.

Montpaillard, by the way, is fictional.

CHAPTER II: The terrible year was 1870, the start of the Franco-Prussian War. The treaty of Frankfurt concluded it a year later.

Near the end of the chapter, Allais has Arabella call her cousin Albert, rather than Hubert. I corrected this lamentable error.

CHAPTER III: Sarah Bernhardt was not only a highly respected actress, but a regular member of the Bohemian groups Allais frequented in his youth.

CHAPTER IV: The hapless Parju (Ovide) is a *garde champêtre*, for which there is no exact Anglo-American counterpart: a combination of village constable, game warden, and forest ranger. He is appointed by the mayor, and takes his orders from him. He is not affiliated with the gendarmerie, or with the national police. I'll just call him a village constable, to make things easier.

CHAPTER V: The Bérenger laws of 1885 and 1891, named after the judge and politician René Bérenger, established procedures for parole and suspended sentences.

CHAPTER VI: Silvio Pellico's 1832 memoir, *Le mie prigioni*, was a romantic and pious account of the ten years that he spent in various prisons.

Bluette's prowess as a hunter apparently rivaled Nimrod (Genesis 10:9).

The Rabelaisian list of fishing and birding implements contains many traditional devices from various parts of France, which I thought it would be futile to translate. Most of them are different kinds of nets.

CHAPTER VIII: Sebastien Le Prestre de Vauban was Marshal of France at the end of the seventeenth century; he built numerous forts, and strengthened the walls of many cities. Senior centers were a bit out of his line.

CHAPTER IX: The snippet of Baudelaire comes from *Les Plaintes d'un Icare* ("The Complaint of an Icarus"), from *Fleurs du mal*:

Les amants des prostituées
Sont heureux, dispos et repus;
Quant à moi, mes bras sont rompus
Pour avoir étreint des nuées.

The lovers of prostitutes
Are happy, rested, and sated;
As for me, my arms are broken
From having embraced the clouds.

CHAPTER XI: The Place de l'Étoile (now the Place Charles de Gaulle) boasts the Arc de Triomphe. Delphine-Alice lives in a ritzy neighborhood.

Cher is a department in the Val de Loire, named for the river Cher, although "Nord-et-Cher" is as fictional as Montpaillard.

CHAPTER XII: The "two weeks" refers to the mandatory term of military instruction.

CHAPTER XV: *Le Petit Journal* was a popular conservative Parisian daily; it was cheaper than the others, and carried a variety of features such as horoscopes and serials.

CHAPTER XVI: Louis IX, known as Saint Louis, held court under an oak in Vincennes.

CHAPTER XIX: Fresnes Prison, just south of Paris, is France's second largest prison. It's not Montpaillard Prison.

CHAPTER XXV: Staff sergeant Martin may be André Martin of the gendarmerie, 1814-1897. That's just a guess.

CHAPTER XXVI: Ernest Molier founded his famous private circus in 1880, and it remained popular until his death in 1933. It was known for its trick riders, and gave two performances a year to high society subscribers.

CHAPTER XXX: Blaireau was right; Théodore Agrippa d'Aubigné, the sixteenth century soldier and writer, was known for his violence, excesses, and frequent duels. Jean-Baptiste Colbert held several positions under Louis XIV. Maximilien de Béthune, duc de Sully, was a minister to Henri IV.

DOUG SKINNER has contributed articles and cartoons to *Black Scat Review, Oulipo Pornobongo, The Fortean Times, Strange Attractor Journal, Fate, Weirdo, The Anomalist, Crimewave USA, Nickelodeon, Zuzu, Cabinet,* and other fine publications. His book of picture stories, *The Unknown Adjective and Other Stories*, was published by Black Scat Books in 2014. *The Doug Skinner Dossier,* a collection of short works, was also published by Black Scat in 2015.

His translations include *Three Dreams* (Giovanni Battista Nazari, Magnum Opus Hermetic Sourceworks, 2002), *Considerations on the Death and Burial of Tristan Tzara* (Isidore Isou, Black Scat, 2012), *How I Became an Idiot* (Alphonse Allais, Black Scat, 2013), *Captain Cap* (Alphonse Allais, Black Scat, 2013), *Merde à la Belle Époque* (various, Black Scat, 2013), *Selected Plays* (Alphonse Allais, Black Scat, 2014), and *The Squadron's Umbrella* (Alphonse Allais, Black Scat, 2015).

He has written music for several dance companies, including ODC-San Francisco and Margaret Jenkins; his scores for actor/clown Bill Irwin include *The Regard of Flight, The Courtroom, The Regard Evening*, and *The Harlequin Studies*.

He lives in Manhattan, venturing from his garret occasionally to teach music lessons and to perform his music in discerning clubs and cabarets.

Sublime Works by Alphonse Allais
Published by Black Scat Books

"... one of the great masterpieces of humorous literature."

—*nooSFere Littérature*

"...apart from being long-awaited, *Captain Cap* also comes at a timely moment because its ironies are particularly apposite today as we witness global intellectual colonization." — *Leonardo Reviews*

Translated and with an introduction, notes, and illustrations by Doug Skinner, this is the complete, unabridged text of the original 1902 French classic by the peerless humorist, Alphonse Allais. This deluxe edition also features eight uncollected "Captain Cap" stories, plus a "Cappendix" of rare historical pictures. Over 360 pages of absurdist mirth and howls of laughter.

"Allais comes across as a very modern writer, and his work as an experimental enterprise which is exemplary in many ways... it is also quite possible to invoke such writers as Queneau, Calvino, and Borges." — Jean-Marie Defays

This collection of Allais's rare theatrical texts includes original translations — never before published in English — of ten monologues, three one-act plays, and twelve shorter dialogues, skits and burlesques drawn from his columns in such publications as *Le Chat Noir* and *L'Hydropathe*. This delightful compilation by Doug Skinner (with fascinating notes on the texts) is proto-Dada at its most delicious.

"No Oulipian could fail to be enchanted by his essentially ironic tales, in which he juggles the rhetorical and narrative components of writing with rigorous logic and inexhaustibly zany results."

—Harry Mathews

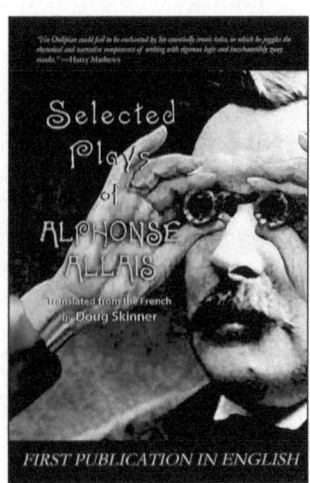

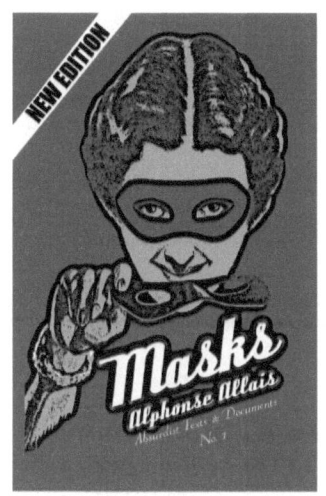

Masks is a darkly humorous, pataphysical tale. It was celebrated by André Breton and the Surrealists, and hailed by the Oulipo. Allais's clever paradox is a prime example of Alfred Jarry's inspired "science of imaginary solutions." This unique edition is illustrated throughout by Norman Conquest and includes a most Allaisian introduction by Doug Skinner, as well as notes on the text.

"A collector's gem." Perfect-bound chapbook in full color. 50 pages. *Absurdist Texts & Documents* No. 1.

"The first and last anarchist in France." — Rachilde

The Squadron's Umbrella collects 39 of Allais's funniest stories — many originally published in the legendary paper *Le Chat Noir,* written for the Bohemians of Montmartre. Included are such classic pranks on the reader as "The Templars" (in which the plot becomes secondary to remembering the hero's name) and "Like the Others" (in which a lover's attempts to emulate his rivals lead to fatal but inevitable results.) These tales have amused and inspired generations, and now English readers can enjoy the master absurdist at his best. As the author promises, this book contains no umbrella and the subject of squadrons is "not even broached."

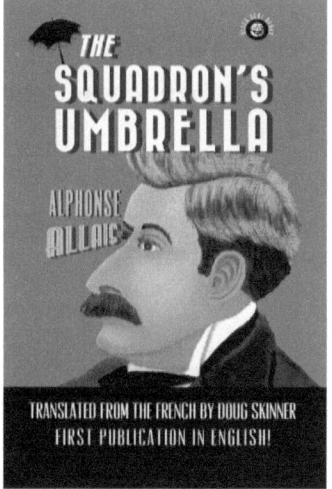

A NOTE ON THE TYPE

This book is typeset in Libre Baskerville, designed by Pablo Impallari, and based on ITC New Baskerville. It is similar to Minion but with a slightly sharper edge.

The title font is Vigneta, an elegant, handmade script created by designer Ilham Henry.